# MAGIC & MISFORTUNE

## STARRY HOLLOW WITCHES, BOOK 14

ANNABEL CHASE

RED PALM PRESS LLC

Copyright © 2020 by Annabel Chase

All rights reserved.

No part of this book may be reproduced in any form or by any electronic or mechanical means, including information storage and retrieval systems, without written permission from the author, except for the use of brief quotations in a book review.

❦ Created with Vellum

# CHAPTER ONE

They say laughter is the best medicine and right now I was in danger of exceeding the dosage. I stood hunched over the kitchen island in Rose Cottage as I swapped childhood stories with my cousins, Linnea and Aster. My side was ready to burst open after their reenactment of a young Florian getting his hand literally caught in the cookie jar. His older sisters had spelled the jar to devour his hand the next time he tried to sneak a cookie.

"Mercy," I said as I tried to catch my breath.

"Oh, good. That means it's time for a present," Linnea said.

"You can't be serious." This would be the fourth gift from them this week. There'd also been a pair of designer shoes, a witchy tote bag with designated compartments for herbs, and an updated grimoire from a celebrity witch called Agatha who was apparently a Very Big Deal in magical circles.

I unwrapped the box to reveal a travel wand. It was retractable and fit nicely in a small purse.

"Isn't it great?" Aster prompted.

"It's amazing and I love it, but please stop showering me with guilt gifts," I insisted. "You have nothing to feel guilty about."

"These aren't guilt gifts," Aster said. "If I see the perfect present for a loved one, I'm going to buy it. Why not share the wealth when we have the money?"

"Those shoes cost more than a trip to DisneyWorld. If it's not my birthday or I haven't solved global warming, then there's no reason to buy me gifts."

They fell silent, their guilt evident on their perfect faces. With their white-blond hair and sculptured features, there was a reason they were easily identifiable as descendants of the One True Witch. Unlike me, who was easily identifiable as a Target shopper.

"My relationship with your mother is separate from the one I have with you. You're not responsible for the rift between us." Aunt Hyacinth and I were no longer on speaking terms, thanks to her destructive need for power and control. She'd been so enraged by my refusal to hand over the magic uncovered from our ancestor, Ivy, that she cut me off, canceled my tutors, and forced my boyfriend to fire me from my job as a reporter at the weekly newspaper. Needless to say, Alec Hale was no longer my boss *or* my boyfriend.

Linnea swilled her wine. "We don't want you to be deprived. You're still a Rose, no matter what Mother says or does."

"I'm not deprived. I have money saved from *Vox Populi* and I'm starting my own business. Everything's still coming up Roses." I smiled to emphasize the pun.

Linnea poured a third round of drinks and shook the empty wine bottle. "I think this is it, ladies. Good thing Sterling agreed to drop us off and pick us up."

"He knows us too well." Aster giggled, a sure sign she was tipsy. My pearls-wearing cousin rarely giggled.

"It's for the best anyway," I said. "Red wine has been giving me a headache lately."

"I've read that can be due to hormonal changes," Aster said.

"Well, I'm not pregnant and it's far too early for menopause, so I'm not sure what hormonal changes they would be."

Linnea swiveled to toss the bottle into the recycling bin and missed. The glass landed on the kitchen floor with a solid thump.

Aster shushed her sister loudly. "You'll wake Marley."

I shook my head. "It would take a lot more than a soft thud to wake her."

My daughter had been asleep for at least an hour. She had a biology test in the morning and was determined to get a full ten hours of uninterrupted sleep. I felt a pang of sleep envy at the thought of uninterrupted sleep. I'd signed those rights away when I gave birth to Marley.

"What if Aunt Hyacinth sees Sterling's car when he comes to get you?" I asked. My cousins weren't brave enough to openly defy their mother. Any interactions with me stayed below my aunt's magical radar or there would be consequences.

"It's dark now," Aster said. "Besides, Sterling glamoured the car when he dropped us off so it looked like a delivery truck. You know Mother has no interest in deliveries. That's for the help to deal with."

I smiled. "Smart."

Linnea polished off her glass of wine. "I wish we didn't have to sneak around."

"You don't have to," I pointed out. "You choose to."

"Can you imagine if Mother knew?" Aster shuddered.

"I appreciate you finding inventive ways to visit me."

"We can't always insist you visit us," Linnea said. "The inn has been busy lately and I'd rather not have to divide my attention. When I'm with family, I want to be solely focused on all of you."

Linnea owned and operated Palmetto Inn, where she lived with her two children, Bryn and Hudson. Despite their magical pedigree, her children had inherited their father's werewolf genes. Linnea and Wyatt Nash were no longer married, but they managed to have a civil relationship for the sake of their kids.

My phone lit up with a text and I frowned at the message.

"Is something wrong?" Aster asked.

"Granger's at the door." According to the text, the sheriff didn't want to knock because of the late hour. He knew PP3 would bark. Prescott Peabody III was my aging Yorkshire terrier with way more bark than bite.

I left the kitchen and hurried to the front door to find out what prompted the presence of local law enforcement.

Sheriff Granger Nash stood on my doorstep, illuminated by the glow of moonlight. His thick brown hair had grown out a bit since I last saw him, resulting in unruly waves, and his defined jawline had more of a nine-o'clock shadow. He wore his uniform, which meant he was here on official business.

"Hey, stranger," I greeted him.

"I found something that belongs to you."

I glanced down to see Raoul, my raccoon familiar, face down on the welcome mat. "Is he conscious?"

"Barely. I found him stumbling around in the street. Once he fell over a third time, I decided to intervene before he became roadkill."

"Is he injured?"

"Only his liver as far as I can tell."

I nudged the raccoon with my foot.

*Pepperoni is my best friend*, Raoul said, sounding dazed.

"Did he get served at a bar?" It was unlikely. Raoul generally sourced his food from the garbage dump, unless I was paying.

"We've had some hot, rainy days recently," the sheriff said.

Every so often, the magical weather bubble that protected Starry Hollow was pierced to let Mother Nature have her way. The most recent piercing resulted in the aforementioned hot, rainy days.

"It's the palm tree berries," Linnea said.

I spun around to face her. "The what?"

"The berries that grow on palm trees. When it rained, the berries fell to the ground and fermented."

I turned back to the sheriff. "He's drunk on berries?"

The werewolf grinned. "Not just drunk. Stupid drunk."

I stared at the raccoon. "I guess I'll carry him to bed and let him sleep it off."

"I drove around with him for a bit to help him sober up, but he kept rolling down the window and threatening to throw up on random residents. I stopped at a red light next to a bus stop and he didn't like the shoes a fairy was wearing. He told her he'd do her a favor and vomit on them so she had an excuse to throw them away."

I stared at him. "How do you know all that? You can't hear him."

"He mimed it. Very interesting choice of gestures, I might add."

I cringed. "I'm so sorry."

"Then he demanded we go through the drive-thru for tacos. He pointed with such force when we drove past, he nearly dislocated his shoulder."

I resisted the urge to smile. That sounded like Raoul. "Thank you for driving him here."

The sheriff eyed me closely. "I can carry him upstairs if you like. You look like you might've been indulging in a few berries yourself."

"Grapes of wrath, but yeah." I motioned to my cousins. "I blame them."

His mouth twitched. "Wouldn't want you to trip while you're carrying him. You'll both be hurting enough in the morning without physical injury."

The werewolf bent down and lifted Raoul, carrying him upstairs like a rag doll. I followed behind him and directed him to the spare bedroom.

"You sure you don't want to tuck him in next to you?" he teased.

"Not if he's threatening to vomit on everyone."

I flipped back the covers and the sheriff placed the raccoon on the bed. He tucked the sheet under the raccoon's chin and smoothed out the creases.

*Half pepperoni and half sausage*, Raoul murmured. *Yes, just like that. More.*

I was relieved the sheriff couldn't hear him. "I think we should leave him in peace before I overhear something I regret."

"You mean he regrets."

"No, I definitely mean me." I hurried from the bedroom and closed the door behind us. "Seriously. Thank you. I don't know what I'd do if something bad happened to him."

"I consider it a public service."

We returned downstairs where Linnea and Aster had made themselves comfortable on the sofa. Aster handed me the glass of wine I'd left in the kitchen and I squeezed between them.

"You're welcome to join us, Granger, although the wine is gone," Linnea said.

"Not when I'm on duty, but I appreciate the offer. Enjoy the rest of your evening, ladies."

"Tell Wyatt I need Hudson's cleats for tomorrow," Linnea said. "He keeps forgetting them."

Aster gave her sister a gentle smack. "Granger is not his brother's keeper."

"Somebody ought to be. He needs one." Linnea's eyes were glassy now and she looked in danger of falling asleep on the sofa.

"I'll send him a text," the sheriff said as he exited the cottage.

"Talk about a keeper," Linnea said. She emitted a deep sigh. "Oh, Ember."

I recoiled slightly. "Oh, what?"

She patted my leg. "He's still crazy about you."

"Because he delivered a drunk raccoon to my doorstep? You've got the crazy part right."

Aster wore a knowing smile. "Trust us. If Raoul wasn't your familiar, Granger would've driven him to the woods and left him sleeping on a pile of leaves."

I gave an adamant shake of my head. "No. He's the sheriff and he's the most kind-hearted, compassionate paranormal I know. He'd do the same for anyone."

Linnea's smile was smug. "You keep telling yourself that, sweetie." She swiped the glass of wine from my hand and drank the rest.

"We're just friends," I insisted, feeling unreasonably irritated. Probably the effects of the wine.

Aster glanced at her phone. "Sterling is on his way. Thanks for a fun evening."

"Thanks for sneaking over. I appreciate the effort."

Linnea embraced me. "One of these days we'll all be back at Thornhold for Sunday dinners."

"Not if your mother has anything to say about it." And she

basically had everything to say about it given that Thornhold was her house.

"We'll wear her down," Aster assured me. "Give us time."

"Your mother is harder than glass. It would take centuries to turn her into a soft grain of sand." And I wasn't certain I wanted to reconcile under the circumstances. Aunt Hyacinth had hurt me deeply. It would take far more than an apology to make things right between us.

"You'll always be family," Linnea said. "No matter what."

Aster stuck out her arms and wiggled her fingers. "Group hug."

Yep. She was tipsy all right. Aster was normally wound pretty tight so this was a refreshing change.

Aster sniffed my hair before releasing me. "You smell like beef stew."

"Weird," Linnea said.

"Not really. I tried to heat leftovers for dinner and ended up using too much magic. The bowl exploded." I shrugged. "I thought I managed to clean it all up, but I didn't have time to shower."

Linnea snorted. "No wonder Granger is so drawn to you when you walk around smelling like that."

Aster suppressed a laugh. "She wears eau du boeuf."

My head was pounding by the time Sterling arrived to whisk them away. I dragged myself upstairs and stopped to check that Raoul was still breathing. The raccoon was now positioned sideways and tucked inside the pillowcase, using the pillow as a mattress.

"Drunk on berries. Who does that?" I murmured.

Shaking my aching head, I closed the door.

# CHAPTER TWO

*What are you doing still in bed?*

I opened my eyes to see Raoul looming over me. "This is not the way I want to wake up in the morning."

*It was either this or let you sleep until noon and we have too much work to do.* Raoul nudged me with all four paws. *Come on, sleepyhead. Time to make the donuts.*

I turned onto my side. "I need more rest. I was up early and took the dog out." And then crawled straight back into bed.

*You can't sulk for the rest of your life.*

"I'm not sulking. I'm sleeping. Or I was before I was rudely interrupted." Relenting, I peeled back the covers and stood. "Where's PP3?" The Yorkshire terrier was usually positioned somewhere on my bed when I was in it.

*On the sofa. That dog sleeps more than a bear in hibernation.*

"He's old. He needs rest too."

Raoul scrambled to the floor. *Marley left for school. Bonkers went with her.*

"Did she eat breakfast?" I asked as we ventured downstairs. Lately Marley had decided she wasn't hungry in the mornings, which did not compute. I usually woke up ravenous and felt nauseous until I ate.

*She took a banana and said she'd eat it on the way there.*

It was better than nothing.

I entered the kitchen to see Marley had made a pot of coffee and tidied up the mess I'd left the night before. I didn't deserve her. I poured a mug of coffee and sat at the table, where Raoul awaited me like a CEO granting an interview.

*I've decided on a name for our new enterprise.*

I snorted. "USS Enterprise?"

He glared at me from beneath his furry brow. *R&R Investigations.*

"R&R makes it sound like we're a railroad."

*Does not.*

"Or that we're in the business of rest and relaxation." Which I didn't object to.

Raoul rolled his beady eyes. *It stands for Raoul & Rose.*

I glanced at him. "Or Rose & Raoul. What about Ember & Raoul?"

*Then it's E.R. We don't want clients to associate us with the hospital. That's too negative.*

What had become of my life that I was taking marketing advice from a raccoon? "Fine. R&R Investigations it is."

*That way if Marley ever wants to join the family business, we don't have to order new business cards.*

"Marley is going to cure cancer or be the first witch on the moon. She won't be joining any family business."

Raoul whistled. *You sure you want to set a bar that high for your kid? That's a lot of pressure.*

"She puts more pressure on herself than I'd ever be capable of."

*What about our logo? I envision a slice of pizza with a magnifying glass over pepperoni that looks like an eye. That tells the client both what we do and what kind of payment we accept.*

"I hate to break it to you, but we are not accepting payment in the form of pepperoni pizza."

The raccoon leaned back and assessed me. *This is a partnership, remember?*

"Money is a smarter business decision because it's more versatile. Money buys pizza and also pays bills."

He folded his arms and huffed. *Fine. Play the versatility card. But that pizza box can also double as a notepad, so you're basically getting food plus office supplies. I consider it a win.*

"I think we need a less...unique logo." Marley was my budding artist. I'd ask her for suggestions after school. "Before I forget, you should give the sheriff a thank you gift."

*For what?*

"He found you stumbling in the street last night. You could've been killed if he hadn't brought you here."

*Huh. I was wondering how I got here. I had a dream I floated on an island of trash in the ocean.* He tapped his paw on the table. *So should I wrap you up with a bow and leave you on his doorstep?*

"Haha. You're hilarious."

*I think I'll go rummage now before rush hour. The early raccoon gets the best treasure.*

I was curious to see what he'd unearth for the sheriff at the dump.

After he left, I drank half a cup of coffee and tried to make it to the shower, but exhaustion won out. I fell asleep at the table and awoke an hour later to the sound of PP3 barking. Someone was at the door.

I wiped the dried saliva from my cheek and dragged myself to the front door. If Raoul was too lazy to let himself back in, he was going to find himself on the wrong end of a metamorphosis spell.

Flinging open the door, I said, "If you had any decency,

you would crawl through the kitchen window instead of making me get up."

The shifter on the doorstep blinked rapidly. His build was slight and he had a thick head of reddish hair streaked with gold. Definitely not a raccoon.

"Is...that the client entrance?"

I grimaced. "No, of course not. Sorry about that. I thought you were someone else."

"Someone who climbs through the kitchen window?"

"It's a long story."

"Are you Ember Rose?"

I fidgeted with the knots in my hair. "Yes."

"My name is Ben Bridges. I was told you might be able to help me."

Sweet baby Elvis. He really was a client. I was mortified. Raoul was right—I had to get myself together. No more weekday naps.

"Sorry about this." I swept a hand in front of myself. "I haven't been feeling well."

"I can come back another time. I would've called first, but I didn't have a number. I was given your name and address."

Good thing we were in the process of getting business cards printed.

"It's no problem at all. Please come in."

PP3 watched him warily from the end of the sofa and started to growl. He was none-too-pleased with our visitor.

"Wereleopard?" I asked.

"Cheetah."

Close enough. "I sensed cat, but that's as far as I got."

Ben nodded at the aging dog. "I'm not sure he's happy with my presence."

"He's not staying for the meeting." I scooped up the aging dog and carried him into the kitchen. I grabbed a treat from the jar and dropped it in front of him. Closing the door behind me, I returned to the living room and motioned for Ben to sit.

"I should've scheduled an appointment. This is very unprofessional of me." The werecheetah chose the chair adjacent to the sofa.

I laughed as I flopped onto the sofa. "I'm wearing sweatpants and a T-shirt that says Hex the Patriarchy. I don't think you need to worry about appearing unprofessional. How can I help you?"

He clasped his hands over his knee. "I'd like your help locating a missing family heirloom."

"Why don't you tell me everything you can?" I glanced around for a notepad and pen. Marley usually left them scattered around the cottage. My gaze landed on the pizza box that I'd failed to dispose of. Sighing, I tore off the lid and grabbed one of Marley's thin purple markers. Very professional.

"It's an aquamarine ring that belonged to my grandmother."

Someone stole an old woman's ring? Monster. "Did they steal it from her house?"

"No. She gave it to me to use as an engagement ring." He broke into a broad grin. "I recently proposed to my beautiful girlfriend, Lindsey."

"Congratulations."

"Thank you. We had our engagement party on Friday night at Basil because it's the restaurant where we met. She went to the restroom and took off the ring to wash her hands. When she went to pick it up off the basin, it was gone."

I sucked in a breath. Talk about a crime of opportunity.

"I feel awful. Not only does Lindsey not have a ring, but it's been in my family for generations. My grandmother kept it locked away in the family vault. It took years to convince her to let me have it."

"What changed her mind?"

"She's softened a lot in the past year. She used to be extremely tough." He shuddered. "I mean full-on whacks with the rolling pin when you displeased her."

"I have experience with tough older relatives." Although I couldn't imagine Aunt Hyacinth holding a rolling pin, let alone wielding it as a weapon.

"Good, because all my relatives are pretty tough." He tugged his earlobe. "That's what's so upsetting about this. We rented the whole restaurant for the party."

"I see. Is it possible someone else thought they'd eventually inherit the ring from your grandmother? Maybe they were upset to see Lindsey wearing it?"

He shrugged. "It's possible. From what I've heard, the bulk of her estate is going to the family of her first husband. I'm her grandson from her second marriage, but I've had my eye on that ring since I was a little boy. I guess she decided to give me the piece of family history I wanted instead of some random painting."

"Does the ring have sentimental value for her?"

"I assume so. Nanny Berta never wore it and I've often wondered whether she associates it with her first husband. He died in a tragic accident."

"That would certainly taint it for her." I understood that kind of pain, having lost my husband Karl in a tragic accident too. "If she never wore it, how did you even know about it?"

"I glimpsed it as a boy when she and my father were arguing over it. He'd taken it from the vault and Nanny became angry. Not rolling pin angry, but worse. I was afraid she might shift right there and then."

"Do you remember why they were arguing?"

He shook his head. "I was too mesmerized by the stone to pay attention to what they were saying. It's the most gorgeous pale green color you've ever seen. It puts all other rings to shame."

It sounded like quite a jewel.

He balled his hands into fists. "I want that ring back. Lindsey deserves a ring as stunning as she is and Nanny Berta…" He averted his gaze.

"What about her?"

"Nanny was so upset when she found out the ring had been stolen…" His expression grew pained. "She suffered a stroke. She's in the hospital now and they're not sure when they'll be able to release her."

No wonder he wanted to find the ring. Ben was probably carrying around a measure of guilt.

"I suspect she isn't going to last much longer. I'd like her to know the ring is back in safe hands. Anything to make her feel better."

"Any idea who else was in the restroom with Lindsey at the time?"

"It was busy. It happened between dinner and dessert, so they all seemed to go at the time. There was a washroom attendant, but she says she didn't see anything."

I wrote a few notes on the cardboard.

"Just out of curiosity, can I ask who recommended our services?" We hadn't started advertising yet.

"Alec Hale."

I swallowed my shock. "How do you know Alec?"

"I don't. He overheard Lindsey and I talking about it at the coffee shop. I said how uncomfortable it would be to interview my relatives and he suggested I get in touch with you. Said you have a special way of getting paranormals to open up."

How ironic that Alec was the one to tell him that.

"He's my former boss at the newspaper." I omitted the boyfriend part. I had to block out the personal element or I wouldn't make it through the remainder of the meeting. "I'd like a list of everyone who attended the party." I'd also go to the restaurant to speak to the staff.

Ben took my purple marker and cardboard and made a list. "I'm only putting the family members I suspect."

"Do you think that's wise to rule the others out? Wouldn't you rather leave that to me?"

"Tensions are already high because of the wedding and certain family dynamics. I don't want to exacerbate them. Besides, I know my mom wouldn't have taken it, so I'm not putting her on the list and Lindsey's family doesn't know anything about the ring other than it now belongs to her."

He passed the cardboard rectangle back to me. There were enough names to get me started. If I needed the others once I finished, I'd finagle them.

"This is great. If I could just get a deposit from you..." I told him the amount.

Ben's head bobbed. "Absolutely." He paid me cash. Perfect. "Will you keep me updated?"

"Absolutely." I gave him my phone number and added his to my contacts.

I waited until Ben left to let the moment sink in. My first official client.

Now that I was a business owner, I had to look the part and that meant showering. I felt a renewed sense of energy. Aunt Hyacinth wasn't going to destroy me. She was only going to make me stronger.

When I finally returned downstairs, Raoul was there with a thank you present for the sheriff.

"What did you find?"

Raoul stuck out both paws. A small red object was

clutched between them and I moved closer to examine it. A plastic fire engine? No.

"Raoul, you cannot give the sheriff a squeaky toy as a thank you gift!"

*Why not? Dogs love them. Watch.* He tossed the fire engine to the floor and stomped on it to make it squeak.

PP3 lifted his head, glanced at the toy, and lowered his head again.

"Yes, it's clearly a huge hit," I said.

*Don't worry. I have a Plan B.*

"I hope it's not a leash."

The raccoon scurried outside and returned a moment later. I smiled at the sight of the tarnished trophy with a plaque that read *You're Pawsome*.

"Much better." I scratched his head. "I have good news." I told him about Ben's missing ring.

*We really need those business cards.*

"I'm asking Marley to come up with a design when she gets home. We'll have them printed straight away."

On cue, the door swung open and Marley staggered inside, dumping her backpack on the floor like she'd carried it through the Andes for the past six weeks.

"School is like a job," she declared.

"And now I have another job for you." I told her about the need for a logo.

"At least that's a fun job."

"Since when is school not fun for you?" Marley excelled in every subject. Curiosity was her drug.

"It's fun, but I hate having to stick to the curriculum. Every time I try to expand the discussion, the teachers drag me back to the book."

Ah. That sounded more like Marley.

I noticed two beady eyes over the crest of her cloak pocket. "What's that?"

She glanced down and pulled the stuffed toy from her pocket. "A raccoon doll. Isn't it adorable? One of my friends gave it to me because it looks like Raoul."

The raccoon climbed down from the chair to inspect the doll up close. *Are you kidding me?*

"What's wrong? It's cute."

*Am I joke to you people?* He flicked the doll with an annoyed paw. *That looks nothing like me.*

I laughed. "It's a raccoon. How could it not look like you?"

He gaped at me. *And what? All raccoons look alike? Is that what you're saying?*

"What if I dressed him in a little cloak and a pointy hat?" Marley asked.

Raoul slapped a paw over his eyes. *I'm going to find a doll that I think looks like you two. See how you like being mocked.*

"No one is trying to mock you," I insisted.

He punched an angry paw in the direction of the doll. *That thing tells another story.*

Marley stared at the doll, fully aware that Raoul was not as enamored as she was. "I'll keep him in my room so he doesn't bother you."

*His very existence bothers me.*

"And I'll name him something completely different." She paused. "Like Raj."

Raoul gave an exasperated cry and ran from the room.

Marley hugged the doll to her chest. "Well, if you ever want to get rid of Raoul, you know where to find this little guy."

# CHAPTER THREE

BASIL WAS an upscale restaurant tucked away on an attractive side street with fey-lit lampposts and cobblestone sidewalks. Alec and I had eaten here once, but he wasn't a big fan of the menu so we didn't come back.

I strode up to the hostess stand where an elf was chatting with one of the servers about a sporting event. I stood politely for a moment, but it became clear they were too wrapped up in their conversation to notice me.

Finally I'd had enough. "Hi. I'd like to speak with the manager."

The server scurried away as the elf's gaze flicked over me. "Sure, Karen."

"My name is Ember."

He made a noncommittal noise.

Oh, it was like that, was it? I was tempted to bust out the Rose name, but I was actively avoiding using the name to my advantage given the current state of affairs with my aunt. I opted for a different approach.

"I'm interviewing suspects in connection with a theft that occurred at this restaurant. Perhaps I should start with you."

His thin eyebrows lifted. "I see. Let me check if he's available." He swiveled on his heel and darted into a back room, returning a minute later. "Kevyn can see you now."

Kevyn was a tall reed of a man whose species took me a second to identify. A wingless pixie. I wasn't sure whether it was because he'd lost his wings, had a birth defect, or was only half pixie. In any case, it would be rude to ask so I didn't.

"Kevyn, I'm Ember Rose of R&R Investigations." I handed him my new business card, complete with a logo of a raccoon holding a magnifying glass to study a set of paw prints. I was only mildly miffed not to be represented in the image. "I'm investigating a theft that occurred here a few days ago."

"Yes, the aquamarine ring."

"My client spoke to you about this?"

"If by spoke to, you mean did he rant and rave like a lunatic and upset other patrons, then yes. He spoke to me."

I had a hard time picturing soft-spoken Ben ranting and raving. It didn't seem to be in his nature.

"He mentioned there was a washroom attendant in the restroom at the time of the theft, as well as other guests. Can you tell me their names?"

"I can identify the attendant, but the guests are unclear. As you can imagine, we don't keep security cameras aimed at the restroom doors."

"Who's the attendant?"

"Her name is Kathleen. She's working now if you'd like to speak with her."

"Thanks, that would be great." I eyed the plate of gnocchi and Brussels sprouts on his desk. "That looks amazing, by the way."

"It's divine. Our chef has been upping his game recently."

"I don't even like sprouts and I want to eat that."

Kevyn smiled. "Then he's done his job."

I tore myself away from the food that wasn't mine before I did something embarrassing. Pushing open the restroom door, I peered inside. The stalls were empty and a lone woman sat on a stool beside the row of sinks. A basket of towels rested on her lap.

"Hi. Are you Kathleen?"

She frowned at me. "Yes."

I let the door close behind me. "Hi. My name is Ember Rose." I produced another business card and handed it to her. "I'm investigating the theft of a ring that occurred here a few nights ago."

Kathleen nodded solemnly. "I feel terrible. That poor young lady. Not a great start to a marriage, I'll say that much. Very ominous."

I wasn't superstitious enough to believe that.

"Did you see the ring when she placed it on the basin?"

She shook her head. "She placed it on the far end of the basin closer to the door. I didn't have a clear view of it from this position."

I pivoted toward the door for a view of the other basin. "Do you happen to remember what the other guests looked like who were in the room at the time?"

"I've been trying to remember, but it seemed like they all converged at once. I do remember a woman with a thick brown braid though. She was head and shoulders above the others. Tall enough to be an Amazon. Wore a white dress, which I thought was disrespectful." She wrinkled her nose in disdain.

"Thanks. That's helpful." I paused.

"But I don't think the Amazon swiped the ring."

"What makes you so sure?"

"Because she was at the sink closest to me," Kathleen continued. "She would've had to walk past the young lady and reach for the ring before leaving the restroom. It would've been obvious."

Although if the restroom was as busy as everyone said, Lindsey wouldn't necessarily have registered the tall woman's movements.

"Thanks for your help."

Kathleen sighed. "I wish I had seen the ring. Sounds beautiful."

"Someone else thought so too, apparently."

"If you ask me, the young lady's a fool for taking it off. If I had a ring as precious as that, they'd have to pry it off my cold, dead body."

"She was probably afraid that it might slip off and fall down the drain." I knew someone that happened to back in Maple Shade, New Jersey. She was able to call a plumber to retrieve it from the pipes, but it was quite an undertaking and she was loath to remove the ring after that.

"I hope you find it. She was a pathetic thing, on her hands and knees with her dress hiked up, scouring the floor." Kathleen pressed her lips together. "No lady should cry on the day of their engagement. It's bad luck."

"I would think losing a family heirloom is worse luck."

Kathleen smiled. "Fair enough."

I exited the restroom and returned to Kevyn's office. "Who were the servers for the engagement party?" Maybe one of them knew more about the alleged Amazon. Despite Kathleen's recollection of events, it still seemed important to speak to her, if only as a witness.

Kevyn scraped the last of the gnocchi from his plate and I felt a pang of food envy. "Terrence and Wanda. They're my best servers." He consulted the clock on the wall. "They're here now in fact."

"Perfect." My stomach gurgled. Maybe I'd grab a quick bite while I was here. It would be nice to have a restaurant I

MAGIC & MISFORTUNE

liked where there was no chance of running into Alec. Starry Hollow was a small town and I needed to carve out space for myself.

I requested a table and was seated in Wanda's section. The redheaded fairy fluttered from table to table, carrying trays of food and drinks with remarkable speed and agility. She'd clearly been doing this a long time. She spotted me at the table and darted over.

"Welcome to Basil. First time?"

"I've been here once before."

"Well, I hope this is the beginning of a new era. Can I get you something to drink?"

"First I'd like to ask you about a party you worked the other night. Ben and Lindsey Bridges."

"Right. The future bride and groom. They were quite the family."

"How so?"

She popped a hand on her hip. "I've seen their type before. Lots of money means lots of problems. I've got no money and one kid is all the family I need."

I smiled. "You sound like me." Or the human me, anyway. "How old is your child?"

"He's six. His name is Ollie. He's a great kid." Concerned lines creased her forehead. "That reminds me. I need to check on him. His dad picked him up from school early because he wasn't feeling well and brought him to his place."

"Ugh. That's the worst. At least his dad is in the picture. I used to have to rely on a neighbor in our apartment building."

A faint smile touched her lips. "Yeah, silver linings, right?" She nodded to the menu on the table. "What can I get you?"

I didn't need to look at the menu. I placed my order and let her take it to the kitchen before interviewing her. Right now I wanted the gnocchi and sprouts more than I wanted answers. Priorities. Across the room I spotted another server. Terrence. I caught his eye and waved him over.

"What can I get you? Water?" Like Kevyn, Terrence was a wingless pixie. Interesting.

"I was hoping to speak to you about an engagement party the other night."

His face rippled with understanding. "The ring, right?"

"Yeah. I was hired to investigate."

"I didn't see anything. I was on drinks duty, so I was too busy to notice any shenanigans unless they happened between the bar and the tables."

"And did you notice any…shenanigans?"

Terrence smirked. "The usual. Paranormals who can't hold their liquor. Feuding relatives. Couples who are only fake happy. The second they let their guard down, you see their bitterness and resentment rise to the surface."

"Any indication which feuding relative might steal a ring?"

"If I knew, I would've told them. Sorry."

I slipped him a card. "If you think of anything, will you get in touch?"

He smiled at the card. "Cute raccoon."

"He's my business partner."

"Hey, I'm not judging. I get enough weird looks as a pixie without wings."

"Kevyn too."

He nodded. "It's how I got this job. We met at a rehabilitation center. He lost his wings in an accident and I lost mine from a genetic disease."

"I'm sorry to hear that."

"That's life, right? You play the cards you're dealt. I like my job and Kevyn's a great boss, so I can't complain." He rested his hands on the edge of the table and leaned in. "Now

I have a question for you. Why didn't your client go to the police? Why hire a P.I.?"

My mouth opened but no answer came out. It was a good question and one I hadn't considered.

"Maybe it's because they stole it from someone else, so they can't go to the police," he continued.

"It's a family heirloom. The grandmother kept it locked in a vault for decades until she gave it to Ben."

"Why did she keep it locked in a vault for so long? Maybe it's because she's been waiting for the heat to die down on her stolen item, huh?"

"I'm not sure it was worth stealing if she waited this long to pass it on."

He shrugged. "Food for thought."

"Speaking of food," Wanda's voice rang out. She set a plate in front of me.

"I'll let you dig in," Terrence said and went back to work.

Wanda lingered. "I guess you spoke to Terrence."

"Yeah. He didn't notice anything."

"Me neither. Like I said, I've been doing this a long time and I've seen their type before, but I didn't see anything to suggest one of them would take off with the engagement ring. It's pretty ballsy."

I agreed. So which relative was the ballsiest? I'd have to talk to Ben again.

Just as soon as I finished my meal.

When I called Ben, he asked me to meet him at the hospital where his grandmother was still recovering from her stroke. He thought it might be good for me to meet Nanny Berta and ask her any questions I had.

"Ember, I'd like you to meet Lindsey."

"Nice to meet you." I smiled at the petite werebadger. She

had copper-colored hair and the kind of toned arms that made me want to rush home and do fifty tricep curls. Scratch that. It made me want to *look* like I'd done fifty tricep curls.

"And this is Nanny Berta." Ben patted his grandmother's hand. "Sorry. She's not exactly lucid at the moment. I was hoping she'd be in better shape, but she seems to have taken an unexpected turn today."

"Hi, I'm Ember," I said to the older woman. Her eyes stared vacantly into the abyss. A shiver ran down the length of my spine.

"This is the lady I hired to find the ring, Nanny," Ben said in a loud voice.

"Any updates?" Lindsey prompted.

"The restroom attendant remembers a woman in the bathroom when Lindsey was washing her hands. She described her as tall like an Amazon and wearing a white dress, which she thought was inappropriate for someone else's engagement party."

Ben and Lindsey exchanged knowing glances. "Lynda," they said simultaneously.

Ben pivoted to me. "Lynda is Nanny's daughter from her first marriage. I put her on your pizza box."

Lindsey's brow furrowed at the mention of the pizza box.

"Yes," I said quickly. "I remember her name from the list." I looked at Lindsey. "Do you recall seeing Lynda in the restroom with you?"

"Not really," Lindsey said, "but I'd had a few glasses of champagne by then, so my powers of observation weren't exactly their sharpest."

"Did either of you interact with Lynda during the party? Did she seem normal?"

Ben grunted in amusement. "Depends on your definition of normal. Lynda is a bit of an oddball. She makes her own essential oils."

I narrowed my eyes. "Need I remind you you're talking to a witch?"

Ben held up his hands. "Okay, but Lynda is a shifter. We don't do essential oils."

"I have another question. Why not take this to the police and let them investigate? Why hire me?"

Ben gestured to the woman in the hospital bed. "Nanny told me not to go to the police. Said they can't be trusted to do the job right."

I felt insulted on the sheriff's behalf. His reputation was pristine.

At that moment, a druid healer entered the room. "Good afternoon. I see we've decided to ignore the two-visitor rule."

I held up a hand. "I'm the guilty party. Ben asked me to come and ask Nanny Berta questions about a missing ring."

The druid's face softened as he gazed at the patient. "I'm not sure she'll be able to answer questions."

"Because of the stroke?" I asked.

"Well, that and the dementia. Even before the stroke, she wasn't always answering the question you asked. When I asked if she wanted me to contact her next of kin, she asked me to contact Arthur."

Ben cut a glance at me. "Arthur was her first husband."

I frowned. "Nanny Berta has dementia? Did you know about that?"

Ben paused. "Not exactly."

"Please don't tell me you took advantage of your grandmother's senility to get your paws on the family heirloom."

His cheeks grew flushed. "No, it isn't like that. I knew she'd been acting...unlike herself, but I thought she was just getting soft in her old age. That she changed her mind about the ring because she realized she didn't have much time left. I swear I didn't know. I wouldn't have taken advantage of her." He looked past me at his grandmother, helpless in bed. "I wouldn't have accepted if I'd realized, Nanny. I'm sorry. I know how special the ring is to you."

"Why didn't anyone tell you about her condition?" I asked.

The druid cleared his throat. "I can answer that one. Her next of kin asked that we keep the information private. He didn't want to upset the family unnecessarily."

Ben pressed his lips together. "That sounds about right. My dad thinks we're delicate flowers incapable of handling tough news. When Grandpa Jack was sick—Nanny's second husband—my dad didn't tell me until he took a bad turn. By the time I got to the hospital, he was dead."

"I'm sorry. That's terrible."

"Dad thought he was protecting me." Ben glanced over his shoulder at Lindsey who had retreated to the corner with a book. "Promise me we'll never hide things from each other to spare the other's feelings."

"Promise, babe." She blew him a kiss.

I inched closer to the bed and took another look at the older woman. Her skin sagged along the jawline and around the mouth. Her pale blue eyes stared back at me, still blank.

The druid ticked a box on the patient's chart. "I'll leave you for now, but try not to let anyone see there's three of you in here. I'm not big on breaking the rules. They exist for a reason." He swept out of the room with his chart tucked under his arm.

Lindsey looked up from her book and it was only then I realized it was a wedding planner. "I'll stay here. No one can see me from the hallway."

Suddenly Nanny Berta seemed cognizant of her visitors. "Ben, what a wonderful surprise."

He kissed her cheek. "Good to see you, Nanny. How are you feeling?"

She squinted. "Uneasy."

Interesting response.

"Mrs. Bridges, my name is Ember. I'd like to ask you a few questions about the engagement ring, if you don't mind."

She stared at me blankly. "Engagement ring? You mean my emerald?"

"No, ma'am. The aquamarine ring you gave to Ben for Lindsey."

"Aquamarine?" Her eyes widened as the realization settled in. "No! How did it get out? That isn't meant for him. It isn't meant for anyone."

Ben edged closer. "Nanny, you told me I could have it. You got it out of the vault."

"I would never do that," she insisted.

He stroked her arm. "You did. I never would've taken it otherwise."

"I don't remember." Tears streamed down the old woman's cheeks and the heart monitor began to bleep incessantly. "Why don't I remember?"

"You had a stroke, Nanny," Ben told her.

"Mrs. Bridges, what can you tell me about the ring's history?" I asked. "Is there a reason another family member might've taken it?"

Her fingers curled around my wrist and she yanked me forward. "The ring," she said in a guttural voice that sounded more like it belonged to an angry troll under a bridge than a frail old woman. "Must. Get. The ring."

Her expression was so intense, it wouldn't have surprised me if she'd ended the statement with a raspy 'my precious.'

She collapsed back on the pillow and closed her eyes. Suddenly the machines around us sprang to life and all started beeping at once.

Ben moved closer to her. "Nanny?"

I was swept aside as a team of healers rushed into the room. Helplessly I watched as they tried in vain to revive her.

"Nanny, please don't go," Ben said, his voice cracking with emotion.

Minutes ticked by, but Nanny Berta didn't wake up.

The druid healer turned to face him wearing a sorrowful expression. "I'm afraid she's gone, Mr. Bridges. We did everything we could."

Ben swallowed hard. "This is all my fault," he whispered. "I upset her too much. If I hadn't lost the ring, she'd still be alive."

The druid clapped him on the shoulder. "Don't blame yourself. Her health was already failing. It was only matter of time."

Lindsey stood and looped an arm through Ben's. "She lived a long life, sweetheart."

"We're supposed to live long lives. She should've had years left." Poor guy.

Lindsey kissed his cheek. "I'm here for you. We all are."

Ben continued to observe his grandmother. "She's going to miss the wedding."

"She'll be there in spirit," Lindsey said. "She was thrilled for us and we'll have the ring to remember her by." The color drained from her face as the words registered. "I mean…"

Ben rounded on me. "Find the ring, Ember. Please."

"On it." I couldn't bear the pained look on his face. I would pry that ring off the finger of the Goddess of the Moon herself if that's where I found it.

# CHAPTER FOUR

LYNDA BELGRAVE WORKED as an acupuncturist downtown. I'd never had acupuncture, but I decided to take one for the team and subject myself to the tiny needles in the hopes of gleaning information about the missing ring. I hadn't expected to get an appointment so quickly given the death of Nanny Berta, but Lynda had an opening so I took it.

"You must be Antonia Fluffernutter," Lynda greeted me. I thought it was best to use a fake name because Rose was too recognizable.

Shaking her hand, I had to crane my neck to look at her. The restroom attendant wasn't kidding about her height. "And you must be Lynda."

The werecheetah gave my grip an appraising glance. "I sense a bit of weakness in the muscles there. Do you lift weights? It might help."

"If by weights, you mean full bottles of wine, then yes. Yes, I do."

She laughed. "Why don't you strip down and position yourself face down on the table? I'll be back in a few minutes."

"I'm glad this isn't a date."

"Are you funny when you're uncomfortable?" She waved a hand. "Not to worry. I see it a lot." She closed the door behind her.

I undressed and tossed my clothes onto a nearby stool. I knew I should probably fold them neatly to give her the impression I was a neat and orderly paranormal, but ultimately I was too lazy to fake it. I was here to find out whether she was a thief, not whether she had standards.

I climbed on top of the table and twisted and tugged the blanket up over my butt. They really needed to create a way to pull up blankets from a facedown position without straining a muscle.

I heard a soft knock on the door. "Are you decent?"

"That's a loaded question," I called back.

The door cracked open and she slipped inside. "Why don't you tell me about your problem areas?"

"Family life. Romantic life." I paused. "Life."

She laughed. "Oh, I know just how you feel. Sometimes it seems like my life is just a series of unfortunate events." She eyed my shoulders. "I can see you're slightly out of alignment. Let me see if I can reduce some of the knots for you."

I swallowed a gasp as she produced long, thin needles. Was she seriously going to stick those in my skin and expect me to feel *better*?

"I'm not surprised by the tension," I said, seizing an opening. "My family is the bane of my existence right now. All sorts of drama happening."

"Oh, sweetie, I feel that so hard." She stuck a needle in my back. "What I hope you don't feel is that."

"It's fine." It was. I expected it to pinch or pierce or *something*, but it was barely noticeable.

"I'm the black weresheep of my family, so I know all about that kind of tension."

"Me too. My parents are dead and I was disowned by my aunt."

Another needle sank into my back. Pretty soon I'd resemble a porcupine.

"My parents are dead too. My mother died yesterday, in fact."

I craned my neck to look at her. "I'm so sorry, Lynda. What are you doing at work?"

She shrugged. "If I don't work, I don't pay my bills."

If she'd stolen the ring for money, she'd be singing a different tune—unless she was biding her time so as not to arouse suspicion.

"My dad died years ago and my mom remarried and had more kids. You know how that story goes. I became an afterthought rather than a member of the family."

"My aunt tried to steal a family heirloom from us," I said. "My daughter and I." Aunt Hyacinth had used us to unlock our ancestor Ivy's powerful magic and then wanted the possessions back so she could reap the benefits. Tough. The heirloom no longer belonged to her.

Lynda strategically placed another needle along my shoulder blade. "That's so crazy. We had a family heirloom go missing too, right in the middle of an engagement party."

"That's terrible. Do you think someone in the family took it?"

Her hesitation was noteworthy. "I suppose that makes the most sense."

If she'd taken it, it seemed unlikely she'd bother to mention it unless she was desperate to bond with me. Even so, I sensed she was withholding information.

"I warded my property to keep my aunt from coming in and taking anything," I volunteered.

"One of the perks of having magic. I think that's why the ring was stolen. It has magic."

I turned my head to the side and rested my cheek on the table. "That's cool. What kind of magic?"

She snorted. "Supposedly it grants the wearer eternal love."

Was that the reason Ben wanted it as an engagement ring? I didn't recall him mentioning it.

"You don't believe it?" It seemed odd for an acupuncturist who made her own essential oils to scoff at the magical properties of a ring.

"I'm willing to believe it's magic, but I'm not convinced it's eternal love."

"Why not?"

"The ring belonged to my mother who was madly in love with my dad. After he died, she took off the ring, stashed it away, and never wore it again."

"Sounds like eternal love to me."

"Did you miss the part where her true love died? She was so beside herself, she settled for a lesser shifter to avoid being alone with her pain. Daddy Bridges was a decent paranormal, but she didn't love him even half as much."

So maybe Lynda had taken the ring in anger—because it hadn't bestowed the gift it promised?

"It doesn't sound like the ring promises immortality," I said. "Only eternal love and, from what you've told me, your mother had that."

Lynda contemplated my remark. "I guess you're right. I never thought about it that way before. I just don't think it's such a hot idea."

"Eternal love?"

"No, using magic to force a connection. If your love is real, you don't need a pretty magical rock to anchor you to your beloved because they're not going anywhere. What's that saying? If you love someone, let them go. If they return, they were always yours. If they don't, they were never yours to begin with."

"Are you happily married?"

She laughed. "Depends on which day you ask me. Most of the time, yes."

"Any kids?"

"We have two. Our older son—that's Theo—is married. Very successful. They live in a gorgeous townhouse near the Painted Pixies. No kids yet, which I think has caused some issues between them. His wife is older than he is and that doesn't help matters. My husband and I have told them to stop putting so much pressure on themselves. We're not royalty. There's no rush to produce an heir and a spare. Our younger son isn't married, but he's got himself a steady boyfriend now and they seem real happy."

"It must make you sad to have lost a family heirloom, especially in light of your mother's death."

"That part is a shame, but if it's a member of the family who stole it, then I guess it's still technically in the family. I'm not saying it's right that someone took it, but it's not as bad as some random thief smuggling it out of the restaurant to sell it on the black market."

The black market. It hadn't occurred to me to check where the ring might be sold. I'd have to research where the likely places were. Then again, Lynda seemed fairly confident that the thief was a family member. Was it because she knew more than she was letting on?

"All the needles are in. I'm going to let you rest for a bit and then I'll be back to remove them."

I didn't relish staying in this position for any longer than necessary. Although it didn't hurt, it wasn't comfortable either.

While she was gone, I ran through our conversation again

and put myself in Lynda's shoes. Who would she want to protect other than herself?

The answer came easily. I'd throw myself in front of a moving train for Marley. I expected Lynda was the same. If her younger son was happy in his current relationship, it had to be Theo. The question was—why did she suspect her son in the first place? She said he was successful, but if they believed the ring brought the wearer eternal love…Was it because she knew they were having marital problems or because she knew for a fact he'd taken it?

An image flashed in my mind of Theo's name in purple marker on the pizza box right below Lynda's. Yep. Definitely a suspect worth talking to, but probably best not to mention it to his mother given my current status. Those needles might not hurt now, but I bet she could find another place to stick them that wasn't as therapeutic.

The door opened and Lynda poked her head inside. "How do you feel? Ready for a nap?"

If only. I had far too much work to do.

Theo and Stefany Belgrave lived in an attractive brick townhouse within walking distance of downtown. The shiny black door was decorated with a wreath of brightly colored flowers that smelled incredible. I was so distracted by the scent that I nearly forgot to knock. I only remembered when a neighbor entered the townhouse next door and gave me a lingering look.

"I'm not casing the joint," I told the nosy neighbor. "I'm here on business."

The elderly man glowered at me before pushing open his door. I was half tempted to tell him I was a prostitute, but that seemed unfair to the Belgraves.

When I noticed the neighbor still watching me, I made a

show of ringing the bell. Only then did he enter his house and close the door. Sheesh. Talk about neighborhood watch.

The door in front of me opened, drawing my attention back to the business at hand.

"Hi, are you Theo?"

He was an attractive werecheetah with a head of tousled blond hair that could've indicated laziness, but he wore it so well that it didn't matter. He wore a collared shirt with the top three buttons open, exposing thick tufts of hair on his chest. I imagined the look was quite appealing to other shifters.

"I am. Can I help you?"

"My name is Ember Rose from R&R Investigations." I handed him a business card.

His brow furrowed as he read the card. "A private detective? What's this about?"

"I understand you attended Ben and Lindsey's engagement party at Basil."

"That's right. What's this about?"

"You didn't hear about the missing ring?"

He scratched the side of his head. "No. I left early. What happened?"

"Someone stole the bride-to-be's engagement ring."

His eyes widened. "Nanny Berta's aquamarine ring?"

"That's the one."

He blew out a breath. "Holy hellhound. Nobody told me." He waved awkwardly as his elderly neighbor made another appearance. "Why don't you come inside?"

I stuck out my tongue before entering the foyer of the traditional townhouse. The floor was made of wide-planked oak and a grandfather clock lorded over the entryway.

"Can I offer you anything to drink? We have sparkling water infused with pretty much any flavor you can think of."

"Rum raisin?" I had no idea why that flavor popped out of

my mouth. My father had been a huge fan of rum raisin ice cream, but I hadn't thought about that in years.

Theo gave me a curious look. "Um, maybe not every flavor."

"I'm fine, thanks."

"Why don't we sit down in the living room?"

I followed him to the seating area and chose a comfy oversized chair. Theo made himself comfortable on the sofa. A large framed photograph of Theo and presumably his wife hung over the fireplace.

"Why did you leave the party early?" I asked. "Sounds like it was a nice event other than the theft."

He glanced away. "I was tired. I'd worked late and didn't feel like hanging around."

"Was your wife with you?"

His stony expression answered me first. "She was."

"How early did you leave?"

He drummed his fingers on the arm of the sofa. "We didn't finish dinner."

Hmm. According to Ben and Lindsey, the ring was stolen between dinner and dessert.

"Your wife left with you?" It seemed more likely that a woman had been the one to take it. As busy as the restroom was, a man would likely be noticed there.

"She did." He frowned. "But she wouldn't have taken the ring. She has plenty of nice rings."

"Maybe she took it for some other reason." I paused. "Or for you? Some family members seem to believe the ring has the power of eternal love."

He snorted. "Yeah, I've heard that story. Not sure how believable it is. Why lock the ring away in a vault if it has magic like that? I mean, who doesn't want eternal love?"

I pinned him with a hard look. "Exactly. Who doesn't?"

He squirmed uncomfortably. "Fine. We left because my

wife and I had an argument and thought it was best to leave before we made a scene and ruined the party, but we're certainly not at the point where we'd steal poor Lindsey's engagement ring. That's nuts."

"Would you mind telling me what the argument was about?"

"Uh, yeah. I mind very much. It has nothing to do with a missing ring." He snapped his fingers. "You should talk to Erika."

I remembered the name Erika from the pizza box. "Who is she?"

"A cousin. She's a werepanther though. Didn't inherit the werecheetah genes."

"What makes you suggest I talk to her?"

"I saw her ogling the ring when she was having a conversation with Ben and Lindsey. They were talking about travel plans, but I noticed Erika kept staring at the ring. She even made a joke about how she could buy her entire college education with that ring. Lindsey seemed embarrassed. She moved her hand away after that and turned the rock inward so the stone wasn't visible."

We were so engrossed in our conversation that we failed to hear the front door open and close.

"Who's this?" a voice demanded.

Stefany Belgrave stood at the edge of the living room. Unlike the smiling woman in the framed photograph, this Stefany had a slightly downturned mouth that made her seem perpetually sad or disappointed.

Theo turned to address his wife. "Hey, hon. I didn't realize you were home."

"I'll ask again. Who is this?" She spoke slowly, her tone laced with suspicion and jealousy.

Uh oh. I was suddenly glad I hadn't used the prostitute joke earlier. We needed to set the record straight pronto. I wasn't keen on getting into a tussle with a werecougar, no matter how much older than me she was.

I jumped up from the comfy chair and strode toward her, holding out a business card. "My name is Ember Rose. I'm a private investigator."

Her hands flew to the curve of her hips. "Did he hire you to follow me?"

"Why would I need to do a thing like that?" he asked. "Do you have something to hide?"

I was beginning to regret my decision to interview Theo in his house. Lynda wasn't kidding about their marital issues.

Theo rose to his feet. "You're bored with me, aren't you? You've decided to trade up. You want someone with more life experience. Maybe that guy from your floral arrangement class. He's closer to your age."

Stefany gaped at him. "Jordan? You can't be serious."

"You can tell me, Stef. I don't want to cling to someone who doesn't want to be with me."

The werecougar shook her head in disbelief. "Gods, you can be such an idiot. How could you possibly think I'm tired of you? I love you more than anything in the world."

Relief doused his features. "You're sure? You've been so distant lately. I thought maybe…"

Stefany dropped her purse on the floor. "I'm a cougar, baby. You know I like 'em young."

"Thank the gods." He wrapped his arms around her and held her close. "Why have you been so distant?"

She kissed his cheek and withdrew from his embrace. "The healer found a lump. I've been waiting for test results to find out if it's…" Trailed off, she wiped a stray tear from her cheek. "I've been so terrified of dying and leaving you behind. I knew it was a risk when I married someone younger, but I didn't think I'd be confronting my own mortality so soon. I thought if I pulled away from you now, you'd be more willing to move on if I…I didn't make it."

He held her shoulders. "And?"

She broke into a smile. "Tests were negative. It's a benign lump."

He planted a kiss on her lips. "As if I could ever move on from you. You're the love of my life, Stef. There's no one else in the world for me."

I felt incredibly uncomfortable intruding on their private moment. "I'll just let myself out," I whispered.

Based on what I learned and the timing of their departure, I was fairly confident they had nothing to do with the theft of the ring. I crept toward the door, but they didn't seem to notice. They were too wrapped up in each other. In light of Stefany's confession, I had a feeling they'd be mastering conception any day now. As thrilled as I was for them, I had no desire to witness the miraculous event.

## CHAPTER FIVE

Cleaning was not one of my strengths. Still, I wanted to set a good example for Marley and that meant keeping the cottage free of cobwebs and other signs of neglect. Although I could've used magic, I'd been avoiding its casual use ever since I discovered the full extent of the abilities I'd acquired from our ancestor, Ivy. I worried I'd intend to blow dust from a shelf and end up blowing a hole through the wall instead.

With earbuds firmly in place, I danced around the cottage to the up-tempo beat of Billy Joel songs as I dusted and tidied everything within reach. I even disposed of the empty pizza box and transferred the list of suspects to an actual sheet of paper and the notes app on my phone in order to appear more professional. By the time Marley arrived home from school, she'd barely recognize this place. I dusted and straightened the objects on my altar, which hadn't been touched in weeks and the signs were beginning to show, especially the moldy piece of bread I left there. Oops.

I whipped around to dance my way toward the dining table when I noticed PP3 jump to the floor with the energy of a puppy on cocaine and run to the door. He sniffed along the perimeter like he was trying to scent a bomb.

I removed my earbuds and stuffed them into my pockets. "Who's coming, buddy?"

A low growl emanated from the aging Yorkshire terrier. Hmm. Not a good sign. Then again, PP3 was wary of most visitors. He was old, but he'd protect Marley and I any way he could, even if that meant peeing a circle around us and declaring that territory off limits.

I opened the door as Deputy Bolan exited his vehicle. Ah, that explained it.

"Hey, green goblin. What brings you here?"

He folded his arms as he approached the doorstep. "Green Goblin was played by the very handsome and charming Ryan Reynolds. I take that as a compliment."

Mimicking him, I crossed my arms. "That's Green Lantern. Willem Dafoe played Green Goblin."

The leprechaun paused. "Is he handsome and charming too?"

"He has an interesting face."

The deputy winced. "That's the kiss of death."

"He's enjoyed a wonderful career as a character actor." I made a sweeping gesture. "Welcome, esteemed member of law enforcement."

The deputy looked at me askance. "Are you drunk?"

"While I don't necessarily disapprove of day drinking under the right circumstances, alas no. I was cleaning and listening to music."

He surveyed the interior of the cottage. "I think you missed a spot."

I craned my neck. "Where?"

He waved a hand airily. "Everywhere. All the spots."

"Not everyone is as fastidious as you." I once watched the

leprechaun use not one, but two gloves to touch a doorknob after someone sneezed in the next room.

That's two gloves on the same hand.

"I'd offer you a drink, but I know you'll want to inspect the cleanliness of my kitchen before you accept."

"I'm not from the health and safety department."

"No. I think you missed your true calling." I scooped up PP3 who was currently pawing my leg. "What brings you here other than an overwhelming desire to criticize my housekeeping?"

He heaved a sigh. "I don't love this part of the job."

"Bureaucracy? I thought paperwork pumped through your veins."

"Not that." He inclined his head toward the big house. "Family drama."

I frowned. "Aunt Hyacinth sent you here? Why?"

"She claims you're running a business out of your house which is a housing violation. Rose Cottage isn't zoned for business or multipurpose. It's strictly residential."

I closed my eyes and mentally counted to ten. "Let me get this straight. That witch had my boyfriend fire me from my job and now she's trying to get me in trouble for pulling myself together and earning a living?"

Despite the close proximity to Thornhold, she couldn't eject us from Rose Cottage because I'd inherited it from my parents. Like it or not, the property belonged to me.

The leprechaun hiked up his trousers. "I don't like it either, but technically she's right. If you're going to run a business, you need to find somewhere else to do it."

"Can I apply for a variance?"

"You could, but I can tell you right now your aunt would file an objection. Your best option is to lease an office."

"Like I can afford to lease an office." I'd need a security deposit and probably two months' rent money.

"For what it's worth, I tried to talk her out of it. So did the sheriff."

I blinked. "He knows?"

"Yeah, she called a meeting with both of us."

"But Granger sent you to talk to me," I said, more of a statement than a question.

"It was the sheriff's opinion that Hyacinth was deliberately trying to send him here to twist the knife because of your…special friendship."

I sat on the arm of the sofa and stared at him. "She was trying to weaponize the sheriff against me too." First Alec and now Granger. What was next—getting Marley kicked out of school? No, that would reflect poorly on *her*.

"I'm sorry, Rose. I know this must be a hard time for you."

I glared at him. "No, don't do that."

"Do what?"

"Pity me. Now I'm uncomfortable."

"You don't want me to be nice?"

"No, it's weird. You and I don't play nice with each other."

He straightened his little shoulders. "Fine. Suck it, Rose. Get yourself an office or cease operations unless you want to incur a steep fine." He pivoted on his tiny heel and started toward the door.

Great. More money I didn't have.

Glancing over his shoulder, he added, "You didn't hear it from me, but there's a place available for lease and it's real cheap. Talk to the realtor, Poppy Wise-Sandalwood."

"Why is it…" He closed the door. "…cheap?"

I guess I'd have to find out on my own.

After the deputy left, I called the realtor and then took PP3 for a walk outside to let off steam. I inspected the herb garden and checked the strength of the ward around the property. Every time I thought my aunt had calmed down, she lobbed another grenade. When would it end?

PP3 let loose one of his happy barks. I turned in the direction of the driveway to see Florian approaching on horseback.

"She isn't home," he said. "I thought I'd take the opportunity to come and see you."

"She isn't home because she's out finding ways to make my life difficult again."

He dismounted and bent down to scratch PP3's belly. "Welcome to the club."

I arched an eyebrow. "She still pays for your lavish lifestyle and doesn't thwart your plans. Trust me, we're in different clubs."

"She *constantly* thwarts my plans. Just last week I tried to buy a new car and she blocked the purchase."

"Because you change cars like most paranormals change underpants." I could hardly feel sorry for him. Even his boat was nicer than my cottage.

"I hate to say it, but Mother excels at trench warfare. You won't be able to advance a few feet without one of her magical bombs exploding in front of you." He gave me an appraising look. "But if anyone can challenge her, I'd say it's you."

"You really think so?"

He nodded. "She's only pushing so hard because she's afraid of losing."

"Why is everything win or lose with her? Why can't she accept the situation with grace and not hold it against us?"

"Put yourself in her shoes. You may be a Rose, but you weren't raised as one. The importance of our heritage was hammered into her from a young age. Our power. Our civic duty to those less powerful. Now suddenly she sees herself as the less powerful one and it destroys her idea of herself. She questions her whole identity."

My eyebrows crept up. "Has she told you all this?"

"No, Simon and I have been analyzing her over bottles of ale and fried pickles."

"That's very specific." But also surprisingly insightful. Despite his good looks, Florian wasn't all flash and no substance. "Does Simon think she'll eventually ease up on me?"

Florian met my curious gaze. "Do you want the reassuring answer or the real answer?"

That would be a no then. "Got it."

"I don't suppose you're willing to throw down your wand? I miss you and Marley at Sunday dinners."

"Throwing down my wand means giving in to her unreasonable demands, so no. I won't be capitulating."

Florian appeared resigned. "Fair enough."

"I need to go in a minute. I have an appointment to check out office space. Want to come?"

"How hot is the realtor?"

"No idea, but her name is Poppy Wise-Sandalwood. Do you know her?"

He stood and stretched. "I do. She's a little crazy, but that can be fun. I'm in."

I nodded to the horse. "Don't you need to bring him home?"

He patted the horse's side. "Nope. You can find your own way, can't you, Candle?"

The horse took off. If only paranormals were that obedient.

"Is this office space for your new business?"

"It is. Your mother reported me for operating a business out of my residence."

He grunted. "So your response is to lease an office?"

"I can't think of an alternative. Can you?" I headed to the cottage with PP3 in tow.

"Are you sure this is the path you want to take? It isn't too late to back out."

I cut a sideways look at him. "What's wrong with this particular path?"

"Can't you find another job as a reporter? You seemed to enjoy it."

I halted in my tracks. "Wait. Is my new job too *low brow* for you?"

Florian hesitated, but I saw the truth of it flicker in his eyes. My cousin was embarrassed.

"I used to repossess cars for a living, Florian. In New Jersey." And repossessing the car of an unhappy mobster was the reason I was now in Starry Hollow. Jimmy the Lighter was none-too-pleased and attacked me on the spot. The intense fear triggered my survival instinct, which in turn triggered magic I didn't know I possessed and alerted Aunt Hyacinth to my existence. Later Jimmy tracked me to the tiny apartment where I lived with Marley and PP3. If it weren't for my trio of cousins showing up and whisking us to Starry Hollow, I'd be dead. I owed my aunt for saving my life, no matter that her actions had been motivated by selfishness and greed.

"I know, but Mother set you up with a respectable job at *Vox Populi*."

"And then took it away when I displeased her."

"But you have all that experience. You can use it to your advantage."

I observed him for a quiet moment. "I never realized what a snob you are." That was strictly true. I knew my cousin was snobby about things like wine and material possessions. What I didn't realize was that he was snobby about his associations too.

"You're more like your mother than I realized," I said.

Two pink spots formed on his structured cheeks. "Gods, you're right. I'm sorry, Ember. Sometimes it seeps out of me."

"Snobbery by osmosis?"

He shrugged. "More or less. Think about it. When you're around it all day every day, you can't help but absorb it."

"Linnea isn't like that."

"Linnea is the eldest and she rebelled at every opportunity."

And the result was an unhappy marriage to Wyatt Nash.

Florian squeezed my hand. "I'm truly sorry and I appreciate that you're willing to call me out on my minotaur shit. It's one of the reasons we get along so well."

"I don't care how important you are in this town. I'm never going to kiss your butt. Not even for front row tickets to Springsteen."

He grinned at me. "And I love you for it, cousin."

I refilled PP3's water and grabbed my purse and keys before leaving to view the office. Florian kept trying to change the songs I selected, which resulted in one firm smack on the hand and one threat of more serious bodily harm.

When we arrived at the building, Poppy was pacing back and forth in front of the door talking on the phone in an animated fashion. She was a short, stout witch with brown hair and a puckered mouth that suggested she was once a smoker. We hovered nearby and waited for her to finish.

"Tell that walking, talking piece of garbage that if he doesn't pay his alimony on time next month, I'm going to hex a pair of his boxers and I'm not going to tell him which ones. Let's see how he and his girlfriend enjoy that." Angrily, she shoved the phone into her purse and burst into a wide smile at the sight of us. "Beautiful day, isn't it? I'm Poppy. I know you, Florian, but who doesn't? And I recognize you from coven meetings, Ember."

I shook her hand. "Nice to meet you. Thanks for arranging this."

"No problem at all. I can't wait to show you this space. I know you're going to love it. Such great energy in here."

Florian and I exchanged glances at her abrupt change in demeanor. He wasn't kidding about the crazy part. But hey, she was clearly single.

Poppy unlocked the door and ushered us inside.

"Deputy Bolan mentioned the lease is cheap." I left the obvious question hanging.

Poppy clasped her hands in front of her. "Yes. There's a bit of an issue with…" Before she could finish her sentence, the entire building began to shake.

"Sweet baby King Kong," I said, once the calm returned. "What was that?"

"Unexplained tremors," Poppy said, her bright smile still fixed on her face.

"What in the hell are unexplained tremors?"

"Exactly what they sound like. There are tremors that are unexplained. They seem to have a magical component, but nobody's been able to identify the cause."

Florian whistled. "You could play that song you're so fond of—*Rock the Casbah*. Really set the mood."

I glared at him. "How many times a day does this happen?" Please say once.

"Six."

Right.

"And there might also be a teensy issue with rodents the exterminators haven't been able to tackle. We even hired someone to perform a spell, but nothing seems to do the trick, hence the steep discount. We think the tremors keep them active."

MAGIC & MISFORTUNE

Inwardly I shuddered. A raccoon familiar was one thing, but rats squeezing their way out of the pipes was quite another.

"I really appreciate you showing me, but it's a hard pass."

Poppy studied me a moment. "You know, there is another option."

"One that doesn't involve regular earthquakes and rodent takeovers?"

"It's not without its own challenge. There's a small plot of land downtown that's zoned for business, but no one's been able to build on it."

"Because of unexplained tremors?"

"No, no problems of that nature."

An idea began to form in my mind. "Can you show it to me?"

Poppy flashed a smile. "What kind of realtor would I be if I didn't?"

After walking several blocks, I realized we were right near the Sheriff's Office. Poppy stopped alongside a small patch of land adjacent to the parking lot.

"This is it."

I stared at the property that was no bigger than the perimeter of Rose Cottage. "This?"

"You can see the problem. It's too small to support a reasonably-sized building. Short of driving a campervan onto it, I'm not sure what you could do, but it's dirt cheap and in a prime location."

She wasn't wrong there, although I wasn't sure how I felt about the close proximity to the Sheriff's Office. How many times a day would I be subjected to Deputy Bolan's grumpy face? Would we pass each other on coffee runs?

Florian observed the property. "You could pitch a tent and host client sleepovers. I bet you'd get a lot of business."

"Hardy har. Not the kind of business I have in mind." But

the mention of the tent gave me an idea. "How much is it exactly?"

Poppy gave me the number. "Obviously there's room for negotiation. It's been sitting empty forever."

"I can make it work."

Poppy and Florian seemed equally surprised.

"Are you sure?" my cousin asked. "This isn't an any-port-in-a-storm situation, you know."

Poppy snapped her fingers. "Oh, a port-a-potty. You'll want to consider that."

Florian cringed. "A port-a-potty? Those rats are looking better and better."

"I won't need a port-a-potty," I said.

Florian laughed. "You're basically a sponge. One tiny squeeze and you leak."

I narrowed my eyes. "Thanks for that visual. I don't need a port-a-potty because I'm going to have indoor plumbing." Among other things.

And I knew just the witch who could help.

## CHAPTER SIX

ASTER MET me at the Caffeinated Cauldron. I'd offered to drop by the house, but she refused. I got the distinct impression she was looking for an excuse to leave the house.

"Everything good at home?" I asked, once we were situated at a table by the window. She'd ordered a mint tea with a splash of inspiration and I'd ordered a latte with a double shot of ingenuity and serendipity.

"The twins are climbing the walls...literally." She shook her head, causing strands of her white-blond hair to fall forward. "They've discovered a spell that lessens the effect of gravity. Not quite levitation. Anyway, they've realized they can use it to climb the walls and they're taking full advantage."

"Sounds like you have your hands full."

"No kidding. Aspen made it to the ceiling with a jar of glitter. You can imagine what happened."

"On the plus side, I bet your living room looked really festive."

She sipped her tea. "Sterling was on a video chat with a

prospective business partner. He wasn't pleased with having a mini-Mardi Gras in the background."

"I'm glad I was able to rescue you from all that." My taste buds fired up once the warm liquid passed my lips. Serendipity offered a nice little kick.

"How's the case coming along?"

"It's essentially a family drama, so right up my alley."

Aster wore a vague smile. "I agree you're well-equipped."

"I still have to find the ring, of course. That's when I'll get paid." I didn't want to share too much about the ring and breach my client's confidentiality.

"I thought you might need help with the case and that's why you asked me here."

"I do need your help, but not with the case." I swallowed another mouthful of my latte. "I'd like to buy one of your sheds."

Aster blinked in rapid succession. "For Rose Cottage?"

"No. Thanks to your mother, I need to lease office space, but I don't have the funds. I did, however, manage to find super cheap land zoned for a business that can't support a permanent structure."

Her mouth melted into a smile. "But it can support a Sidhe Shed."

"Exactly."

Aster brightened. "I'll tell you what. If you'd be willing to keep a sign on the outside of it that promotes the business, I'd be willing to let you have one for free."

I waved my hands in front of me. "I don't want a handout."

"This isn't a handout. This is business. You're going to smack that shed in the middle of a busy section downtown. You'll basically be a billboard for Sidhe Sheds." She flicked out her elegant fingers. "I can already picture the interior. You want it to look professional but also a reflection of you."

"And those two things are polar opposites," I reminded her.

"Don't be silly. I can design storage for your magical items as well as a comfortable seating area for clients."

Her enthusiasm began to rub off on me as I pictured the possibilities. It would be a place of my own, outside of Aunt Hyacinth's influence. A place where I wasn't within view of Thornhold and the power she held over me. It would also allow a clear separation between business and personal time. I'd leave any work at the shed and focus on Marley and my personal life at home.

"The more I think about it, the more I love this idea," I said. "How long will it take to finish?"

"Let me get a few options together first and you can decide which direction you want to go." She hugged me. "I'm so excited we'll get to work together after all."

Aster had invited me to be part of the business when she first started, but I declined, knowing it wouldn't be the right move for me.

"Me too. You have no idea how excited." I'd been so bummed to see the first option, but maybe it was a blessing in disguise.

"I should probably get going. I feel like I can't leave the twins for too long or they'll burn down the house and Sterling will be too busy to notice. He'll end a video chat and realize he's outside."

I laughed. "I'm sure everything's under control."

She blew out a breath. "I feel like I'm raising two Florians, which seems grossly unfair." She finished her drink and left the empty cup. "Talk soon."

I took a minute to finish my drink, feeling upbeat about this turn of events. Finally I stood to leave and walked smack dab into a broad chest.

"I'm so sorry." I looked up into the stoic face of Alec Hale.

"Miss Rose."

So we were back on formal terms. Got it. "Mr. Hale. Nice to see you. Sorry about stepping on your toes. What brings you here?" Alec rarely got his own coffee.

"It's a lovely day. Tanya volunteered to get the coffee, but I decided to take advantage of the sunshine."

I laughed. "Seriously? I know you, Alec. You don't do sunshine."

"Fine. Tanya's been angry with me over what happened and refuses to get the coffee."

Huh. No one told me.

"Would you like me to have a word with her?"

He sniffed. "Certainly not. I'll take care of it."

Taking care of it seemed to mean continuing to get the coffee until her anger simmered down.

I clasped his hand in mine and squeezed. "I'm happy to see you, Alec. You look great." Then again, the vampire always looked impeccable, like he'd been carved from a slab of marble infused with sex appeal.

He squeezed my hand in return before releasing it. "Have a good day, Miss Rose."

My chest tightened as I left the coffee shop. I was going to have to find a new place to lurk if there was the risk of running into Alec every time I craved caffeine. As much as the breakup had been my decision, I didn't want to be reminded of him at every turn. Thanks to Aunt Hyacinth, I was all maxed out on personal drama.

Erika was a werepanther rather than a werecheetah like most of Ben's blood relatives. She was only two years younger than Ben but, according to my research, had taken the scenic route through life and was only now attending college while working part-time at a body piercing shop called Prick. I'd tried to track her down at school, but it seemed she wasn't consistent about attending classes. She was, however, consistent about showing up at work to earn a paycheck. I found her relatable before I even met her.

It took me a few minutes of wandering along the sidewalk to locate the entrance to Prick. There was no sign and I had to venture down a set of concrete steps that took me to a building basement. Apparently Prick was like a speakeasy with bling.

Wearing a black top with strategically placed cut-outs and her black hair in messy Harley Quinn-style pigtails, Erika was easy to spot in the small shop. She was currently in consultation with a customer and the debate seemed to be whether to pierce the right nipple or the left one.

"My left one is more sensitive," the werewolf explained.

"Is your partner right-handed or left-handed?"

"Southpaw."

"Then go for the right nipple."

Another piercer—this one a vampire—was engaged in conversation with two teenagers and I wondered whether they had parental approval. Marley would be grounded until her eighty-third birthday if she got a piercing or tattoo without my permission.

The vampire pointed from one girl to the other. "If you think you might cry, you can both leave right now." He swiveled to point to the sign on the wall that sported a crude sketch of a crying baby in a circle and a line slashed through it. "We don't serve them."

The blonde puffed out her chest. "Got it. I'll go first."

"You're not afraid of needles, are you?" he asked.

"I thought you used guns not needles," the blonde said.

Erika scrunched her nose. "No self-respecting piercer uses a gun."

"Guns are for kids," the vampire said. He seemed to

realize his statement. "Wait. That didn't come out right. Guns are for sissies."

I frowned. "I don't think you got it right that time either."

He turned back to the two young women. "Back when we first opened, I used my fangs until some whiner filed a complaint with the health and safety department."

This was my cue. I swiveled toward Erika. "Do you have a minute, Erika? My name's Ember and I'm a private investigator."

Erika glanced at her co-worker and he nodded. "Let's talk outside."

"Can I listen?" the werewolf asked.

"No," we said in unison.

We retreated to the concrete steps that led to the alley. She tugged an object from her purse.

"Mind if I vape? It's bubblegum."

"Would you mind waiting until we're finished?"

She scowled and stuffed the item back into her purse. "What's this about?"

"Your cousin Ben's missing engagement ring."

She rolled her eyes. "Such a drama llama."

"Someone stole a family heirloom worth a lot of money. I'm not sure hiring an investigator to find it qualifies as being a drama llama."

She folded her arms. "And what? You think I stole it?"

"I'm speaking to everyone who attended the engagement party since that's where the ring was taken." Okay, maybe not everyone, but Erika didn't need to know she was on the shortlist.

"Why would I take that stupid ring? It's hideous." She gestured to her appearance. "Do I look like the kind of girl who would wear a ginormous cocktail ring?"

"I doubt you'd intend to wear it. It would be too recognizable."

She glowered at me. "Oh, I see. I'm a poor relation and, therefore, I must've stolen it in order to make a buck."

"You were seen admiring the ring and someone overheard you commenting on its value. Something about covering your college costs."

Her brown eyes blazed with anger and resentment. "It's true. The system is ridiculous. I have three different loans that I'll have to start repaying as soon as I graduate. No one should have to go into debt to get an education, but I'm not desperate enough to steal anything. That's not my style. Besides, if I stole the ring to pay for school, why wouldn't I have paid off the loans?"

"Because you're waiting for things to calm down before you find a buyer."

She scoffed. "I pierce a lot of fencers. They don't hold anything for long. Stolen goods are like hot potatoes or ticking bombs."

"Would you mind giving me some names? Maybe the thief has contacted some of your connected customers."

Erika bit her lip. "I can't do that."

"I'm not a cop, Erika. I'm only going to ask them questions on your cousin's behalf. Don't you want me to recover your family's heirloom?"

She pulled a face. "I couldn't care less about some stupid ring. Nanny Berta kept it locked away my whole life. It can't be that important."

"It's important to Ben and Lindsey."

She fidgeted. "I honestly don't know anything. I saw the ring at the party and, yeah, maybe I was annoyed that she could wear a stupid object that would cover my entire college education, but I didn't take it from her. I like both of them."

"If you didn't like both of them, would you have stolen it?"

She scowled. "Like I said, it's not my style."

"Where were you between dinner and dessert?"

"Outside vaping. They wouldn't let me do it in the restaurant."

"Can anyone confirm that?"

"The busboy was out there with me. His name was Victor."

That would be easy to confirm.

"Did you use the restroom at any point during the evening?"

She lifted her chin. "No, I did not. Why? Is that where the ring was stolen?"

"It was."

"I have an iron-clad bladder. Years of practice. The lines in clubs are always miles too long."

She wasn't wrong there. I'd used the men's restroom on many occasions just to bypass the line.

"Listen, just because I look a certain way doesn't mean I'm a criminal. Ever hear of not judging a book by its cover?"

"Actually we all judge books by their covers, but not the point. Anyway, I'm not judging you. I'm asking questions based on information I was given."

She folded her arms. "And I've answered them. Anything else?"

"Actually there is. Just out of curiosity, why does it matter whether his partner is left-handed or right-handed?"

She glanced over her shoulder to the interior of the shop. "Oh, it doesn't. I just needed him to make up his mind. I know his type. He's nervous so he can't make up his mind, but he's too cool to admit it."

A scream pierced the air, followed by a dull thud. Erika threw open the door and we peered inside. The blonde was sitting on top of her friend who was passed out on the floor.

She gently smacked the brunette's cheek. "Wake up, wimp. He's done."

"She fainted as soon as I finished," the vampire told us.

"Title of your sex tape." Erika's lips peeled into a smile. "And you owe me money." She cut a glance at me. "As soon as they came in and announced they wanted their belly buttons pierced, I bet on the brunette keeling over."

The vampire shook his head. "Sometimes this job can really surprise you. The brunette looked tough to me. I thought for sure the blonde was going to hurl."

The blond teen looked up at him. "Gee, thanks. For your information, she's the one who cracked a tooth on the toilet seat last week when she passed out from drinking too much."

"Isn't it your job to hold her hair back?" I asked.

"I was, but she was wearing extensions. The comb slid out and her face hit the toilet." She shuddered at the memory. "We had to scramble to come up with a good story for her mom."

I'd love to know how they planned to explain a piercing. Then again, not my circus, not my bedazzled monkeys.

"Thanks for speaking to me, Erika," I said. "If you hear anything, will you let me know?" I handed her a business card.

"I guess," she said in a tone that suggested otherwise.

"I'm sorry about Nanny Berta, by the way. I know how it feels to lose a loved one."

She gave me a brief nod before turning back to her customer. I watched as she slid the card into her back pocket and I had no doubt it would end up in the garbage can the moment I left. Ah, well. It was the cost of doing business.

# CHAPTER SEVEN

Although I was crossing names off the suspect list, I didn't feel as though I was making progress. It was time for a chat with my dear friend, Artemis Haverford. The elderly witch had been around long enough to know the history of every piece of jewelry in Starry Hollow. If this ring truly had magic connected to eternal love, there was a good chance she would know about it.

I parked behind an unfamiliar car in the semi-circular driveway of Haverford House. It was a nice ride, a shiny black Florian-style vehicle with a touch more elegance.

I approached the front door of the historic home. Artemis had lived in the crumbling mansion for decades, along with her familiar, Clementine, and her ghostly manservant, Jefferson. Marley and I adored the elderly witch. It helped that she had no allegiance to Hyacinth and didn't tend to partake in coven events. In fact, as sweet as she was, Artemis was one of the few witches Hyacinth had no control over. If Artemis didn't want to do something, she didn't do it, no matter who was pressuring her. The Rose name meant nothing to her, except in the sense that she considered two members of the family to be close friends.

I entered the parlor room where Artemis was entertaining a handsome guest. I sensed a whiff of magic and realized it was emanating from him.

"Ember, what a wonderful surprise," Artemis said.

I noticed the coffee table was covered in what appeared to be…bones. "I'm sorry. I should've let you know I was coming first." I wouldn't make that mistake again.

"Nonsense." Artemis inclined her head toward the visitor. "Ember, I'd like you to meet a client of mine, Castor Avens-Beech."

A wizard. His dark hair skimmed his shoulders and his lashes were thick enough to braid. "Nice to meet you. I'm sorry to interrupt. I didn't expect anyone would be here."

"You're welcome anytime, Ember. You know that." Artemis signaled to Jefferson. "A fresh pot of tea, please."

A swish of air indicated that the trusty manservant was on the case.

Artemis gestured to the settee. "Do sit, my dear."

I cut a glance at the bones. "I feel like I'm intruding." And I wasn't sure I wanted to know what kind of personal matter required bones.

"It's quite all right," Castor said. "Artemis and I are studying my romantic prospects."

"With…" I motioned helplessly at the coffee table.

"Bones," Artemis said.

"Yes, I figured that much. Who did they belong to?"

"Roadkill." Her puckered mouth formed a smile. "Waste not, want not."

She was using the bones of dead animals found on the side of the road to glimpse the wizard's romantic future. That didn't bode well.

"You're a wizard," I pointed out. "Can't you do that on your own?"

"This type of work isn't in my wheelhouse, I'm afraid."

A tray with a pot and cups floated in and distributed among the three of us. I went straight for the sugar cubes to add to my tea. The sugar aside, there was something about it in cube form that appealed to me.

"Well, you can't go wrong with Artemis." My focus drifted back to the bones. "What would you like the bones to tell you about your romantic prospects?"

Castor adjusted the collar of his shirt with finesse. "I'm ready to marry and I'd like to make sure I'm choosing wisely. Our line depends on a good match."

He sounded like a medieval king choosing his queen. "What makes it a good match?"

"My family's strength is potions. I'd like to balance that out with a witch strong in other areas like psychic abilities."

"You're trying to genetically craft more powerful offspring?"

He chuckled. "Why not? After all, we can't all be descendants of the One True Witch. We need to find alternate means to strengthen our line."

My cheeks burned at the mention of my powerful lineage. "But why seek to strengthen your line at all? What's the point?" This wasn't medieval times when strengthening kingdoms through strategic marriages and children made sense.

Castor seemed taken aback by the question. "Because this is what my family has always done. My father chose my mother on the basis of her family history, as did his father before him."

"They didn't marry for love?"

Castor snorted. "Certainly not, although I'm fortunate in that my parents have great affection for each other."

Great affection? I had great affection for Raoul, but I didn't want to marry the raccoon.

"I know it may seem old-fashioned," he continued, "but it's worked well for my family for generations."

"No inbreeding to preserve the gene pool, right?" As hellbent as Hyacinth was on finding the perfect match for Florian, even she wouldn't consider a blood relation.

Castor cringed. "Certainly not. The situation isn't as dire as that. No one's at risk of losing a head if they don't produce an heir."

"And dating the old-fashioned way hasn't panned out for you?" He was certainly good-looking enough to attract any witch he wanted. With Castor back in town, Florian was going to have competition in the eligible bachelor department.

"I've been traveling the past few years on behalf of the family business, which has taken the werelion's share of my time. Now that I've settled back in Starry Hollow, the time has come to focus on personal matters."

"Any decent prospects so far? I can name a few witches who are single, but I don't think I can rank them by their abilities."

"Never mind, Ember. That's what these are for." Artemis flicked a bone with her own bony fingers.

Castor's smile seemed almost sly, as if he knew a secret he was dying to share. "A few, yes. We'll have to see how things progress. And for what it's worth, I'm sorry about the horrid business with your aunt."

I balked. "Does everyone know our family business?"

"When the family is yours, yes. I'm afraid so." His eyes shone with sympathy. "One look from Hyacinth can shrivel coconuts on a tree. I think you're incredibly brave to stand up to her."

Or foolish. Only time would tell.

"I believe we're finished here. I'll leave you two to converse." The wizard rose to his feet and kissed the old witch's hand before leaning forward to shake mine. "A pleasure."

"It was wonderful to see you again, Castor. Don't be a stranger."

Once he departed, I moved closer to Artemis. "He seems nice and normal for someone with such outdated views on marriage."

"You think so?"

I did. "I guess normal's relative though." With my human history, I probably still seemed strange to half the coven. Okay, ninety-five percent of the coven.

Artemis gazed at me over the rim of her teacup. "I know I'm breaking my own rules of confidentiality, but I feel compelled to tell you that you're an option for Castor."

"An option? You make it sound like I'm on the potential mate shelf at the supermarket."

She laughed. "You're a potential match."

I motioned to the coffee table. "According to your roadkill?"

"Bones are bones, Ember. It doesn't matter where they came from."

"Tell that to the people in *Poltergeist*." I glanced at the bones. "Who else did the bones tell you was a potential match for him? Anyone I know?"

She pretended to zip her lips. "That's all I'm willing to say."

"Well, I don't want to marry Castor. I'll leave him to his other prospects."

"The marriage would be advantageous to both of you. His family is highly respected in town and it would offset the issues with Hyacinth."

"I doubt his family would want the black sheep of the Rose family to merge with theirs. I'd be a black mark on their pristine record. Besides, I'm not even sure I want to have more children and that's obviously a sticking point for them."

"Why ever not? You're still young enough and I'm sure Marley would adore a sibling."

That was the upside of giving birth to Marley when I was so young. She was old enough now to help out if I wanted to bring another baby into the world.

"My life is in a state of flux at the moment, in case you haven't noticed. I don't think I should be making any long-term decisions, certainly not in the romance department."

She reached over and patted my hand. "How are you recovering from your breakup with Alec? It must be difficult for you."

"I'm fine." I withdrew my hand and toyed with the nearest bone. "What if you chuck these bones for me? Do you think I'll learn anything interesting?"

She squinted at me. "Is this a question of love or perhaps one of a more familial nature?"

I dropped the bone. "Never mind. I don't want to know."

"Very well then. What brings you here?"

"I need to ask you about a ring. It seems to have some history behind it and I thought you might know something about it."

"Where did you acquire it? I wouldn't purchase any jewelry from that dwarf on Firefly Lane. It's all fake from what I understand."

"I didn't purchase it. Someone hired me to find it. The ring is a family heirloom and it was stolen from a restaurant earlier this week."

"Oh, I see. How dreadful. And what makes you believe this ring has a history?"

I explained about Ben's grandmother and the claims of eternal love.

"I don't suppose you have a photograph of this item?"

"As a matter of fact, I do." I tapped the screen of my phone and located the image to show her. It was a photo from the party of Lindsey showing off her ring.

The older witch's eyes widened and, for a fleeting moment, I glimpsed the way her face once looked without the deep creases.

"You recognize it?" I wasn't sure why I bothered to ask. Her expression made it perfectly clear.

"Yes, my dear, I certainly do. That pale tint of green is a dead giveaway. I always thought the stone was a myth. A tale you told children to frighten them."

"Who wants to frighten children?" Older generations had a warped idea of fun, although gallows humor was probably the only way to go when you could drop dead of dysentery or the pox.

Artemis shrugged her bony shoulders. "Your generation has its Freddy and Jason. We had our Ring of Despair."

Ring of Despair? Well, that wasn't ominous or anything. I settled back against the settee. "Tell me more about it."

"The story goes that Hera..." She peered at me. "You know who that is, don't you?"

"Greek goddess with a jealous streak? Married to Zeus." And the god was always making sexy time with other women, so Hera's jealousy was understandable.

"Yes, that's the one. Hera was upset that Zeus was spending time with a mortal woman, so she decided to seek a mortal man of her own. Her chosen conquest was a young man named Damon. He was a brave young man determined to prove his love and loyalty to Hera by sailing to an island off the coast to capture a rare beast in her name. Before he and his crew set sail, she gave him a ring with an aquamarine stone, said to be the palest tint of green."

"Why aquamarine?"

"Because aquamarine means water of the sea. The stone is sacred to sea deities. Sailors like Damon believed such a stone would placate them and provide safe passage."

"I'm guessing that didn't happen."

Artemis shook her head. "Hera's plan worked and she got her husband's attention. Poseidon created a vicious storm and sank the ship on behalf of his brother Zeus. The entire crew died, including Damon. Because the sea god himself was the one who sank the ship despite Damon's possession of the sacred stone, it's said to be cursed."

"I guess so with a name like the Ring of Despair. How did anyone find it?"

"Treasure hunters. They search for sunken shipwrecks and bring back their spoils, not knowing what magic they might unleash as a result. If I recall correctly, the ring turned up in Pompeii and was discovered among the ashes after Mount Vesuvius erupted."

That was next-level misfortune.

"Each time the ring makes an appearance in history, bad luck follows," Artemis continued.

"It seems like Ben's grandmother knew the stone was cursed, which is why she kept it stashed away."

"A wise decision, although a better choice would've been to destroy it."

"How does it work? Does it bring bad luck to the one who wears it?"

"No one knows for certain, but it seems to have an impact on more than the one who possesses it. The ship succumbed to the storm, for example, and Damon died, but so did the rest of his crew."

"If that ring is back in circulation, it could be very bad for Starry Hollow," I said, more to myself. "I hope I can find it before it does too much damage."

Artemis gave me a long look. "I hope so, too, my dear. For the sake of us all."

# CHAPTER EIGHT

Armed with the dire news about the missing ring, I decided it was time to seek help from the sheriff. As much as I wanted to handle my first case on my own, it was now a matter of urgency and I had to cut as many corners as possible.

I strode through the entrance to the Sheriff's Office and approached the front desk. "Hi. I'm here to see Sheriff Nash."

The elf behind the desk looked at me with a blank expression. "And you are?"

My fingers curled into a fist. "You know who I am, Dottie. I come here all the time." Dottie only worked part-time, but we'd certainly interacted enough times that she'd remember me.

She arched an eyebrow. "Do you?"

I rolled my eyes. On the one hand, it was sweet that the employees were protective of the sheriff. On the other hand, knock it off.

"Tell him Ember Rose is here on official business." I passed her my card.

She scrutinized the card like she was looking for a hidden

message. "What does R&R stand for? Roles & Responsibilities?"

I swiped back the card. "No. Rose & Raoul."

The elf shook her head. "I'd never guess that."

I pointed to the logo of the raccoon. "He's Raoul."

"And you're Ember. It should be E&R."

I stuffed the card in my purse. "Forget it."

"Oh, you don't want to see the sheriff anymore?" she asked in a sickly-sweet tone.

"Yes, I still want to see him. I just don't want to dissect the name of my business with you."

"Fair enough." She smiled. "Go ahead back."

I marched forward, tempted to tip back her chair as I passed by. I fought the urge. Between my new role and my neighboring office, I'd have to see Dottie regularly. No need to make it less pleasant than it already was.

Hovering in the doorway, I noticed the You're Pawsome trophy on the sheriff's desk. It seemed Raoul had taken the time to deliver his thank you gift. Nice.

I cleared my throat. "Hi. If you have a minute, I need your help." Ugh. I hated asking for help. Just saying the words out loud was a struggle.

He angled his head, examining me. "What kind of help? Are we talking tuck-my-drunk-raccoon-in-bed kind of help or somebody-stole-my-car kind of help?"

"Somewhere in between." I dropped into the empty chair opposite him. "I need a list of paranormals who deal in stolen goods."

He burst into laughter. "And you're asking me?"

"Who else? You know the usual suspects in town."

He fiddled with a pen. "You've hung out your shingle for all of a week and you're already wading into dangerous waters." He clucked his tongue. "Typical."

"I have a very good reason." I told him about the ring and

its dark history. "I think those recent rainy days we had might even be connected to the ring. The timing corresponds to the stone being taken out of the vault and given to Lindsey."

He stroked his jawline, contemplating the possibility. "It was unusual for this time of year, but I didn't think much of it."

"There's a chance that whoever stole the ring will try to sell it if they haven't already." If Artemis was right about the ring's divine and destructive provenance, it was imperative that we find it as soon as possible before *very* bad things started to happen.

"And what makes you think those guys will talk to you?"

I held up my compact travel wand and extended it. "This."

"Magic, huh?"

"No, I'm going to threaten to shove it up their..."

He clamped his hands over his ears. "Come on, Rose. I'm worrying about you already and you haven't even gone to talk to them yet."

"So you think threats of violence are a bad idea?"

The sheriff exhaled. "What do you think?" He picked up his keys off the desk. "Let's go."

"Go where?"

"I'm going with you."

I laughed. "You can't. They won't talk in front of the sheriff. Just give me the list and I'll handle it."

He shook his head. "No dice. I go with you or you don't get any names from me."

I whistled. "Wow. Sheriff Nash playing hardball." Annoying and yet kind of sexy. I pushed myself to my feet. "Then I'll get the names another way. Thanks though."

His mouth dropped open. "You can't be serious."

"I'm not going to get information from criminals with the head of law enforcement as my escort. It'll be fruitless." I slung my purse strap over my shoulder. "I appreciate the offer." I started for the door.

"Rose, wait."

I stopped and slowly turned to face him. "Yes?"

He scribbled on a slip of paper and handed it to me. "Start with this one. She's a major player. If I had hot property that threatened to burn my fingers, she's the first one I'd see."

I tucked the slip of paper into my purse. "Thanks, Granger."

His dark eyes softened. "I don't want to worry about you, that's all. You got yourself in enough hot water chasing stories. Now you're chasing criminals."

I patted his stubbled cheek. "No need to worry. You seem to forget that most of those stories involved chasing criminals."

Before I could withdraw my hand, he reached for it, curling his fingers around mine. "I'm always going to worry about you, Rose. Can't be helped."

Time stretched as we continued to look at each other in silence. He leaned forward and I realized he was about to kiss me. Even more startling, I realized that I wanted him to.

A knock on the doorjamb jolted us and we sprang apart.

"Boss, I have that report you wanted."

I turned to see Deputy Valentina Pitt stride into the office, her ample hips swaying as she approached the desk with a file in her hand.

The sheriff quickly recovered. "Great. You can just drop it on my desk. Thanks."

The curvaceous deputy assessed us. "I heard you mention criminals. Anything I can help with?"

He lit up. "As a matter of fact, there is."

"Not," I added quickly. "There is not."

Deputy Pitt glanced from the sheriff to me. "If Sheriff

Nash thinks you require assistance, I think you should heed his advice."

"Take backup, Rose. It'll make me feel better."

"I appreciate the concern, but it's not my job to make you feel better. That's a You problem."

He nodded. "Fair enough."

Deputy Pitt shook her head. "You're a stubborn witch, aren't you? Let me come with you. I've been writing traffic tickets all morning. I could use a pick-me-up."

I heard myself relent, but only because the fate of Starry Hollow was at stake.

"Terrific," the sheriff said. "Pitt, you're undercover for this. Change into street clothes and accompany Rose."

An idea snapped into place. "You can pretend it's your ring that was stolen."

"Sounds good." She directed her thick lashes at the sheriff. "I like a little role playing. Livens things up."

"I'll bet," I murmured. "I'll meet you out front in two minutes."

"Okay then." Deputy Pitt lingered for another moment before leaving the office.

"She has a crush on you," I said, once she was gone.

"She does not. Deputy Pitt is a young officer of the law and she recognizes my experience."

"She recognizes your nice butt."

He bit back a smile. "You think I have a nice butt?"

I ignored the question. "She's beautiful. She's a werewolf like you. She's even in the same profession. You two are a perfect match. What's holding you back?"

He raked a hand through his dark hair. "Just because two paranormals look compatible on paper doesn't mean there's chemistry. There's more to a relationship than a list of stats."

Tell that to Castor. "She seems to have more than enough chemistry for both of you."

He looked me in the eye. "If that were true, you and I would still be together."

I licked my lips. This was not the direction I wanted the conversation to take. "Granger, chemistry was never an issue. You know that."

His phone buzzed with an incoming text message. "Pitt's in the parking lot waiting for you. Good luck, Rose."

"Thanks." I was relieved to escape the building and our conversation. There were too many emotions competing for my attention and right now I only wanted to focus on finding the ring. It occurred to me that I was doing the very thing that bothered me about Alec—using work to avoid uncomfortable feelings. It seemed the vampire had left his mark on me in more ways than one.

Deputy Pitt didn't have an unmarked car, so I drove us to the address.

"I've never heard of Tupelo Street," I commented.

"Me neither, but I'm still getting to know the town."

"For a small town, there are a lot of nooks and crannies." I turned left and continued along another back road.

"You seem to have settled in nicely, given where you're originally from." The deputy gave me a sidelong glance.

"You know my background?"

"I was curious, so I read your file."

My fingers tightened around the wheel. "I have a file?"

She smiled. "Don't worry. There's nothing incriminating in there, although someone drew a little devil face with horns next to your name."

I smirked. "You can credit Deputy Bolan for that artwork, I'm sure." Or maybe Dottie. Sweet baby Elvis, did they all hate me?

"What can you tell me about the ring? I should probably

know the details since I'm supposed to be the rightful owner."

I shared the photo on my phone, as well as the ring's dark history.

"Wow," she said, once I'd finished. "I didn't realize how serious this was. I thought it was just a pricey piece of jewelry."

"That's why the sheriff wanted to accompany me, but everyone in town knows him. You're new enough that no one will recognize you." They certainly wouldn't forget her though. When a woman looked like Valentina Pitt, she tended to leave an impression.

"The sheriff wanted to accompany you because he likes any excuse to spend time with you."

Saved by the GPS. I pulled in front of a row of quaint brick buildings. At a glance, I saw an antiquarian bookshop, an antiques dealer, and a secondhand jeweler. "We're here."

Deputy Pitt leaned forward to study the buildings. "Which one?"

"The jeweler. Tara's Treasures."

"Doesn't sound like a badass name."

"Which tells me Tara is probably extra badass. This is her legitimate business that hides her illegal activities."

We vacated the car and headed to the entrance.

"I'll take the lead," we said in unison.

We halted and looked at each other.

"I'm the deputy."

"And I'm the investigator. Your boss told you to accompany me, not take over."

Her expression crumpled. "You're right. I'm sorry."

"No need to be sorry. We disagreed and we resolved it. No hard feelings."

She nodded. "It's a bad habit—telling everyone I'm sorry all the time. I'm working on it though."

"That's okay. I wish more paranormals were willing to apologize." In my experience, the ones who *should* apologize —cough, Aunt Hyacinth—were the ones least likely to do so.

The deputy opened the door and I stepped inside the cramped shop. Organization wasn't Tara's strength. The tables overflowed with jewelry and there seemed to be no rhyme or reason to the displays. We must've set off a silent bell because a woman immediately emerged from a back room and stood behind a counter.

"Welcome to Tara's Treasures." The dwarf stood at about five feet. Her rust-colored hair was cut short everywhere except the top where the hair crested like the head of an exotic bird. She wore three necklaces of varying lengths and at least one ring on each finger. I had a feeling Tara treated the shop as her personal jewelry box.

I stepped up to the counter. "Hi, Tara. My name is Ember. I'm working on behalf of my client, Valentina."

The deputy wiggled her fingers by way of greeting.

"Oh, are you a personal shopper?" Tara asked me.

"No, I'm investigating the theft of my client's aquamarine engagement ring."

Tara flinched, but it was hard to know whether she flinched because she knew something about the ring or because she knew I was here about a stolen item.

"And what brings you here?"

"We're canvassing all the local secondhand jewelry stores," I said. "We wouldn't want the ring to be passed on to an unsuspecting customer who believes they're legally acquiring it."

Tara bristled. "All of my items are fully vetted. If your ring was stolen, it wouldn't show up for sale in this shop."

She wasn't technically lying. Tara's dirty dealings likely took place in the back room so the ring wouldn't be for sale in a display case.

"It's a rather large aquamarine stone," I said. "If you'd seen it, you'd remember."

Tara's face became a blank wall. "As I said, I fully vet any pieces that make their way to a display case." She motioned to the nearest table. "If you don't see an aquamarine ring, then I don't have it."

Deputy Pitt threw herself across the counter, weeping. "Please, if you know anything about my ring...It belonged to my grandmother. We were so close. I can't bear the thought of someone outside the family wearing it."

Tara's eyes widened at the sight of the grieving werewolf. She shot me a helpless look and I shrugged. Slowly she reached out to stroke the deputy's head.

"There, there, dear," Tara said. "Your grandmother, did you say?"

She nodded without raising her head from the counter.

"I know how you feel. I was close with my grandmother too. I miss her every day."

"My client has been so distraught, she wants to cancel the wedding. She thinks it's bad luck to get married while the ring is still missing. As you can imagine, it's causing both families a bit of stress. The groom's family is paying a pretty penny for the venue and they don't want to lose all their deposits."

The deputy raised her tear-stained face. "I want to marry him, of course. He's the love of my life. But the marriage will be doomed without Nana's ring. Doomed, I tell you!"

Tara's gaze darted to the door and back to us. "I promise I haven't seen your ring, but I can give you the names of two paranormals who might know."

Deputy Pitt drew herself to an upright position and wiped her crocodile tears. "Thank you. That would be immensely helpful."

Tara lowered her voice. "There's a vampire named Stryder. He owns The Board Room."

The deputy scrunched her perfect button nose. "What's that?"

"He sells board games and offers a space for customers to come and play. Daytime hours are for the under-eighteen crowd and he hosts game nights for adults in the evenings."

"You think a vampire who sells board games might know something about a stolen ring?" I asked.

Tara inhaled slowly, as though debating how much intel to share. "You didn't hear it from me, but Stryder doesn't make the bulk of his income from board games."

I feigned shock. "You don't say."

"The other one you can talk to is a satyr named Jim. He sells memorabilia over on Clover Lane."

Deputy Pitt clutched Tara's wrist with both hands. "Thank you so much for your help. Nana is smiling down on me right now, knowing I'm that much closer to finding her precious ring."

"Best of luck with the wedding, dear," Tara said. "I know this can be a stressful time and I'm sure the stolen ring doesn't help matters."

The deputy flung out a hand. "I'm going to tell everyone at the wedding to shop here for their jewelry needs."

I hustled the deputy out of the shop before she went too far and extended the dwarf an invitation to the faux wedding.

"Impressive performance," I murmured as we returned to the car.

"I excelled in undercover work in Florida. Not much opportunity for it here."

I unlocked the doors and slid behind the wheel. "How did you know to use the grandmother angle?"

She smiled and held up her phone. "The magic of

research. I found an article about Tara when she first opened the store. She talked about how she was inspired by her late grandmother, who had a deep love of jewelry."

"And did her grandmother inspire her to fence stolen goods too?"

The deputy shrugged. "She doesn't mention that." She buckled her seatbelt. "Where to next?"

My phone vibrated with an incoming call from an unknown number. I decided to answer it, thinking it might be related to the investigation.

"Ember?"

I frowned. Although the voice sounded vaguely familiar, I couldn't place it. "Yes?"

"This is Castor Avens-Beech. We met at Haverford House."

I relaxed slightly. "Yes, hi. How can I help you?"

"I was wondering if you'd be free for dinner this week."

I stiffened. Castor was asking me out? It seemed he'd decided to take the information from Artemis to heart. "I'll have to check my schedule and I'm out at the moment. Can I call you later and let you know?"

"Of course. If it would make you feel more comfortable, we could keep it casual. My sister has agreed to join us if you'd like to include your cousin, Florian."

A group outing *was* more appealing. "Thanks. I'll check with him too."

"Thank you. I look forward to hearing from you."

I set down the phone and stared blankly at the windshield.

"Who was that?"

For a brief moment, I forgot I wasn't alone in the car. "A wizard who wants to take me to dinner."

"Aren't you the popular one?"

"Not really. Some chicken bones told him to ask me out."

She gave me a curious look. "Okay then."

I started the car, setting aside all thoughts of Castor. Given my persona non grata status in the Rose family, I was surprised Castor would bother with me. He was clearly aiming to make a socially acceptable match.

"You don't have to worry about me telling Granger," the deputy said. "My lips are sealed."

I jerked toward her. "Why would I worry about you telling Granger?"

"Oh, come on. As much as it pains me to acknowledge it, you two obviously have a thing."

Aha! I knew she had a crush. I was stunned she admitted it though. It seemed like the kind of information she'd want to keep to herself. I'd been desperate to keep my feelings for Alec a secret when I started working at the newspaper.

"The sheriff is a good friend and we care about each other very much."

"Good friends don't look ready to play tongue twister every time they're in the same breathing space."

I pulled onto the road, unwilling to dignify her comment with a direct response. "On that note," I began, "how do you feel about board games?"

## CHAPTER NINE

THE BOARD ROOM was not at all what I expected. I thought I'd see shelves lined with board games and a few card tables scattered around the room where groups could set up Monopoly or whatever game appealed to them. Maybe that was the setup during daytime hours, but the adult game night was something else entirely.

A fully stocked bar was set up at the back of the room and manned by a bartender. A nearby table offered a variety of sweet and salty nibbles. In the middle of the room was a long table that seemed like it would be more at home in a medieval banquet hall.

A lone vampire lorded over the scene in silence. He was average height and wore black jeans with an orange T-shirt that read Mount Doom National Park with an image of the iconic setting in the background. His dark hair was slicked back in a ponytail.

"This place is great," Florian enthused as we sipped our drinks from the bar and waited for the games to begin. "I'm glad you persuaded me to join you."

Deputy Pitt got called away at the last minute. Thankfully

Florian was available and we arranged to meet here. His mother would never come to a place like this so I figured we were safe from her watchful eye.

"Before I forget, do you know Castor Avens-Beech?"

"Of course. He's a little older than me, but we travel in similar social circles."

"He's on the hunt for a wife."

Florian nodded absently. "I imagine his family is pressuring him to have kids."

"I guess you can relate to that."

He looked at me sideways. "Mother's been far too preoccupied fuming over you to pay attention to me. I have to admit, it's been a nice break."

"She'll swing her focus back to you eventually." And probably with a vengeance. Knowing Aunt Hyacinth, Florian would leave his bachelor pad one morning to find a parade of acceptable witches outside Thornhold and his mother would demand that he choose right there and then.

He chewed on the slice of orange from his drink. "I'd much rather be like an old English king and have illegitimate children everywhere than be saddled with one woman for eternity."

I gaped at him. "You can't mean that."

He arched an eyebrow. "Can't I?"

"How would you feel about a double date with his sister?"

Florian leaned closer. "I'm listening."

"It was Castor's suggestion. He thinks I'm more likely to agree if you tag along as my escort."

Florian snorted. "Like you need an escort."

"Are you interested? I'm not, but if you'd like to meet the sister, I'd do it for you."

He brought the cup to his lips. "You know me, Ember. I'm always interested."

"I'll set it up then. Tomorrow night." I turned away from

him to survey the shelves. I needed to get Stryder's attention. "So many games to choose from," I said, a little too loudly.

"Magic chess is a popular choice for adults," Stryder said.

Good. He took the bait.

"Chess is too serious." Chess was a cerebral game that only involved two players. I needed something that would keep a group busy talking and laughing so I could interrogate Stryder without him realizing it.

"Cards Against Supernaturals?" Stryder tapped a box on the shelf. "If your group is irreverent, this one might be the way to go."

"My group is me and my cousin."

"Not to worry. There will be more players soon and you know what they say about strangers."

"Don't accept candy from them?"

"No. Strangers are just friends you haven't met yet."

I fought the urge to gag. "Maybe something more wholesome. Wouldn't want anyone clutching their pearls."

The vampire removed another box from the shelf. "I've got the ideal choice. It's called Guess What?" He set the box on the table and removed the lid. "The cards fit on the front of the hat and the paranormal wearing the hat asks yes or no questions to guess what's written on their card since they can't see it."

"Oh, right." I'd played a different version of the game in the human world.

"You can either create your own cards or use the ones in the box—or a combination of both."

"Are the ones in the box everyday items?" Florian asked, wandering over to join us.

"A mixture. Some are pop culture references. Others are basic words like unicorn and cauldron," the vampire explained.

This would work. "What do you think?"

Florian shrugged. "Suits me. I'm just here for the booze."

"Is it a problem that we've chosen the game before anyone else gets here?" I asked.

Stryder smiled, showing his fangs. "Early bird gets the worm. Such is life."

The door swung open and Wyatt Nash swaggered into the room with a young blonde on his arm. Terrific.

"This is adult night," I said. "You'll want to come back during daylight hours."

Wyatt faked a loud chuckle. "Funny." He gave his date a playful smack on the bottom. "Be a good girl and get us a couple drinks, darlin'."

"So the grownups can talk?" I asked.

"She's plenty legal," Wyatt said.

"Do you just call her darlin' because you forget her name?"

He scowled. "I know her name. It's Ashlee with an 'ee' at the end." He winced. "No, wait. It's Mandee with an 'ee' at the end."

I snickered. "Is this a regular hangout for you? I can see the appeal, all these games aimed for ages six and up."

"This was Mandee's suggestion. She's been here with friends and thought it was a hoot."

Mandee returned with two plastic cups of ale and passed one to Wyatt.

"Mandee, I'd like you to meet my former brother-in-law, Florian, and his cousin, Ember."

"Great to meet you both." Mandee's smile was so wide, I worried about being sucked into a white vortex.

Wyatt rubbed the back of his neck. "I'm surprised to see you two here, to be honest. Doesn't seem like your kind of place."

As I struggled for a response, Wyatt seemed to fill in the blanks on his own.

"Oh, I get it," he said. "This is because of your family rift. You know the big H won't know you're hanging out together if you come to a place like this."

"We have four players," Stryder interrupted. "Why don't we begin and we can add anyone who arrives later?"

We took our places at the table. I was glad I had access to alcohol because this evening was going to be more painful than I expected with Wyatt and his latest girlfriend across from me. I just had to remember the real reason I was here—information. As long as I kept my priorities in order, I'd be fine.

Stryder explained the game to Wyatt and Mandee, as well as another couple who wandered in at the last minute. The pair of trolls seemed to be regulars and greeted Stryder by name. I wondered whether they knew how the vampire really made his money.

"I'll join you for the first round to help everyone get acclimated," Stryder said. He set the blank cards and a marker in the center of the table. "If you want to make up your own options, now's the time. I'll add them to the deck and shuffle them in."

Glancing at Stryder's Mount Doom T-shirt, I grabbed a card and marker and wrote *one ring to rule them all*. Using my travel wand under the table, I murmured a spell that would slip the card to the top end of the pile. One of us would choose this card and it would be the perfect segue to the Ring of Despair.

"I'll be a brave soul and go first," Wyatt offered.

Mandee wiggled her fingers. "Oh, let me, sweetums."

Sweetums? Barf.

Mandee took the card and affixed it to the hat without looking at it. She smiled proudly at us. "Hit me with your questions."

I took one look at the word on the card and shuddered.

"You okay?" Florian asked.

I rubbed my arms. "Just a sudden chill." Thanks to the icy tendrils of fear.

"Ask your first question," the female troll urged. Within the span of five minutes, I learned her name was Gertie and she and her husband, Gary, owned an office supply store downtown. They had three kids, two cats, and their favorite vacation spot was Rainbow Falls. Gary liked to golf, but Gertie found it boring. Needless to say, Gertie and Gary were talkers.

"Is it something I own?" Mandee asked.

"Gods, I hope not," I said.

She placed her hands primly on the table. "Yes or no answers, please."

"Is it something I like?" Mandee asked.

"I would think so," I said. "You're with one now."

Wyatt shot me a dirty look.

As far as I was concerned, they should be banned from existence, but I fully recognized that was my issue.

"I don't know," Mandee said. "Does it fit in my purse?"

"No, but a lot of them can fit in one car," Gary said.

Mandee frowned, uncertain how to interpret that. "Does it spread joy and happiness?"

I cringed. "Fear and loathing, more like."

"It has to be a yes or no answer," Mandee huffed.

"But it isn't. There's a clear divide." Much like politics, clowns could be a divisive issue.

Impatience got the better of her and she ripped off her hat to view the card. "A clown? How is there a clear divide? They're an abomination."

"You cheated," Gertie said.

Mandee flung the hat across the table. "So sue me."

"No point for you this round," Stryder said.

Mandee shot to her feet. "I'm getting another drink."

"She has a bit of a temper," I told Wyatt. "Now I see why you like her."

"Hot tempers do yield certain benefits," he drawled.

"Like what? She goes down for a nap and you get work done?"

He pushed the hat toward me. "Why don't you go next? Keep your mind occupied with something other than my romantic life."

I plucked a card from the pile and stuck it on the hat. "Is it the blue heart diamond from the Titanic movie?"

"We appreciate yes or no questions, but that's oddly specific," Gary said.

"I don't even know what that is—but no," Gertie added.

I pulled a face. "How can you not know?"

"This is Starry Hollow, Ember," Florian chided me. "Not everything popular in the human world crosses the paranormal divide."

"But Titanic," I sputtered. "Kate Winslet's unwillingness to shove over on floating debris." It was the survival version of people refusing to move down the row in a movie theater to make space for newcomers.

They stared at me blankly.

"Whatever," I huffed. "Is it an object?"

"Yes," Wyatt said.

"Bigger than a breadbox?"

"No," Florian said.

"Household item?"

They hesitated. Ooh. I had a feeling this was my card. "Is it powerful?"

"Very." Stryder hesitated. "I mean, yes."

Excellent. Here was my chance. "Is it considered precious to someone in particular?"

A slow smile spread across his face. "Yes."

I brought an enthusiastic fist down on the table. "Is it the one ring that rules them all?"

"Yes!"

We high-fived across the table.

"How weird this ring was on the card. It's almost like the game is psychic." I knew I was laying it on pretty thick, but desperate times and all that.

"Did you just watch the movie?" the vampire asked. "I've seen it a dozen times. The relationship between Frodo and Sam…" He fanned himself with a card.

"I've seen the movies a handful of times, but I'm talking about a different ring that's very precious to me. This one was stolen recently." I snuck a peek at Stryder to gauge his reaction. "It's the most beautiful aquamarine ring you've ever seen."

The vampire's gaze was intense. "You're missing a ring?"

"Yes, and it's very important that I get it back."

"I'm sure everyone feels that way about items that have been taken from them," Gertie said. "I once lost my favorite pair of gloves when we went skiing two years ago. Remember, Gary?"

"No, you don't understand." I kept my gaze pinned on Stryder. "This isn't just a prized possession. This is fate of the world stuff. I'm talking infinity stones."

Stryder straightened. "Infinity stones like in the Marvel movies?"

I nodded solemnly. "Instead of a gauntlet, it's one stone set in a cocktail ring."

The vampire inched his chair closer. "And what does your ring do?"

I dropped my voice. "Spreads misery and misfortune from the point of origin."

"The point of origin being…"

"Whoever has possession of the ring."

His eyebrows knitted together. "So you can't alter reality with it?"

"No."

"Can you control minds?"

"No."

"Teleport?"

I shook my head.

He slapped a hand flat on the table and harrumphed. "Then it's nothing like the infinity stones." Appearing to have lost interest, he turned his attention back to the game.

"I'd like to know more about this ring," Gary said, staring at me wide-eyed.

I forced a laugh. "I was totally kidding." No need to spread panic. "It belonged to my grandmother, but it can't do anything other than make other women jealous at parties."

Hmm. Stryder didn't seem to know anything about the ring. At the very least he might've asked about an association with eternal love because that's the story he would've been told by the thief. It was possible the vampire refused any information about the items he fenced for purposes of plausible deniability, but I got the distinct impression he was clueless about the ring because he didn't have it and never did.

"I'm going to refresh my drink," I announced. I needed to regroup and decide next steps.

I approached the bartender with a friendly smile and set my empty cup on the counter. "Another bucks fizz, please."

Florian left the table to join me and I noticed the concern etched in his features.

"If this ring is as dangerous as you say, why haven't we heard about bad things happening?" he whispered.

I lowered my voice. "We probably have. We just haven't known to attribute them to the ring because we don't know its location. Besides, the ring has only been back in circulation for a brief time. The fact that it was quickly stolen is arguably the effect of the ring."

"This is your client's ring? Ben, right?"

I nodded. "Keep this to yourself, okay? I don't want to set off widespread panic. My goal is to find the ring before it can do too much damage."

"And what will you do once you find it? Return it to the owner? I don't see how that's a good solution."

"I'll fly that broomstick when I come to it." Right now the priority was finding the ring before it lived up to its name.

The bartender leaned forward. "I know I shouldn't be eavesdropping, but you said you're searching for a ring?"

I faced him. "Yes. An aquamarine stone. Have you seen it?"

The bartender glanced over my shoulder in the direction of his boss. "I take it you're here to dig for info from Stryder."

"Someone might've suggested that course of action, yes."

The bartender looked me over. "You don't look like a cop."

"Because I'm not." I slipped a business card from my purse and handed it to him.

He studied the card. "I thought the motto was reading, writing, and arithmetic?"

"Those are the three R's," I corrected him.

The bartender's brow furrowed. "How is that the three R's? It works out to RWA."

"That's the Romance Writers of America," I said. "If you misspell writing and arithmetic, you get three R's."

"Why would you deliberately misspell something?" The bartender rubbed the side of his head. "Now I'm confused." He tucked the card into his pocket.

"Never mind the name of my business. Do you know anything about the ring?"

With one eye trained on the vampire, the bartender

poured another drink. "I see everything that comes through here and there's been no ring that fits the description."

"Thanks. I appreciate the tip." That only left Jim, the memorabilia collector on the list of local criminal enterprises. I'd have to tackle that lead tomorrow before my date with Castor.

The bartender shook his half empty jar. "And I'd appreciate one too."

My cheeks grew flushed. "Oh, of course." I dug into my purse and unearthed a handful of coins, dumping them into the jar.

"Woo hoo, handsome wizard," Gertie called, waving to Florian. "Your turn."

"I think I know why they come here."

Florian took a sip of his drink. "Why's that?"

"They're swingers." I slapped his back. "And Gertie wants to swing with you."

Lucky for me, the only thing Gary wanted to swing was a golf club. I'd take my small mercies where I could find them. If I didn't find this ring soon, though, we'd all be begging for mercy.

## CHAPTER TEN

Clover Lane was more like a back alley than a legitimate road. An offshoot of Cauldron Street, it housed a record store, a comic book dealer, and my destination—the memorabilia collector's showroom.

Jim had the kind of patchy beard that made him look like he landed somewhere between early and modern man on the evolutionary scale. His bottom half was all satyr though. His hooves scraped the hardwood floor as he hurried over to greet me.

"Good day. What brings you in? Looking for an item from a particular movie or television show? If you can name it, I probably have something, even if it's as insignificant as a pen that appeared in season 2, episode 4."

My mind drew a blank. I wasn't expecting to be put on the spot. "How about a TV comedy?"

He crooked a finger and I followed him to another section of the showroom that was stuffed with furniture. He placed both hands on top of a dark purple wingback chair.

"This special chair was featured in episodes of *Friends*.

You might not have seen the show, but it was hugely popular in the human world."

"How did it end up here?"

"I have a network of connections in the entertainment business in the human world."

I eyed the chair. "And where was it featured exactly?"

"I just told you—*Friends*."

"No, I mean where as in which location? One of the apartments? Central Perk? Rachel's office at Calvin Klein?"

The satyr seemed momentarily stumped. "You've seen the show, I take it."

"Every season. More times than I can count."

He scratched his patchy beard. "Um, I believe it was Phoebe's mother's house."

"The beach house?"

He winced. "On second thought, this chair is lumpy and you look like a woman who craves comfort." He moved away from the chair to stand beside a glass coffee table. "This exquisite piece is from a beloved show called *Little House on the Prairie*. Humans loved it. This would be a priceless piece in their world. I can even offer a certificate of authenticity."

I snorted. The only thing authentic in this place was his ridiculous beard.

"I hate to break the news, but there's no way Ma and Pa Ingalls had a glass coffee table in their log cabin on the prairie."

"Oh, no. This belonged to another character," he said, smooth as silk. "A much wealthier one."

"Nellie?"

He smiled. "Why, yes. I believe so."

"Uh huh."

He sensed my misgivings and shifted gears. "Have you heard of *Sharknado*? Another wonderful offering from the human world. This shark replica was used in some of the most famous scenes in the movie."

I frowned at the plastic shark. "I don't think so."

Jim hooked his arm through mine and guided me to a quiet corner of the room. "Listen, I have other customers milling around and you're harshing my vibe."

"And your vibe is what exactly? Hoodwinking innocent shoppers?" I unhooked his arm from mine. "Tell you what. You tell me everything you know about a missing aquamarine ring and I won't tell everyone you're a complete fraud." I gestured to the plastic shark. "Seriously, where did you even get that?"

"From a seafood restaurant in Willow Bend," he muttered.

I rolled my eyes. "Did you steal it or buy it?"

"I pretended to have found glass in my meal and when they offered compensation, I asked for the shark. You'd be surprised the type of items that sell really well. That shark will bring in far more than what the restaurant would've paid me in coins."

I groaned. What a loser. "What do you know about the ring?"

"Aquamarine, you say?"

I nodded. "You might've been told it has an association with eternal love."

Deep lines formed across his brow. "I would remember an aquamarine stone. That's my girlfriend's birthstone. She's a true Taurus, if you know what I mean. If it came to me, I would've given it to her."

"Have you heard about one being sold on the black market? It's a sizable ring. The kind that would inspire chatter."

He shook his head. "I'm afraid not."

Strike three in fencing circles. "Thanks."

MAGIC & MISFORTUNE

"If you're interested in a pair of shoes from *The Wizard of Oz*..."

"Let me guess—ruby slippers."

"No, they're brown boots worn by one of the winged monkeys when he was waiting for his scenes to be filmed."

I squinted at him. "Jim..."

He sighed. "Fine. I bought them for my girlfriend's brother on a sale rack, but they didn't fit and the store didn't allow returns for clearance items."

I patted his shoulder. "Now was that so hard?"

He splayed his hands. "I need to make a living."

"No, you need to make an *honest* living."

"If somebody buys the *Friends* chair and enjoys it, what's the harm?"

"The harm is their joy is built on a lie. It isn't authentic."

"Their joy is authentic. Who cares whether the reason is?"

"We'll have to agree to disagree on that one, Jim. It's a foolish man who builds his house on sand." Or something like that.

"I prefer a fool and his money are easily parted."

My hand made a sweeping gesture. "Clearly. It's your entire business model."

Jim's nostrils flared and he clomped across the room to assist another customer. As I passed him on the way out, I heard him say, "Hey there, friend. Have you heard of a little show called *Games of Thrones*?"


I served leftovers to Marley for dinner, which allowed me more time to get ready for my double date. Just because I wasn't interested in Castor didn't mean I wanted to look like a hag. I generally chose showers over baths, but I decided to use the opportunity to destress and think about the case. Some people I knew in the human world claimed to do their best thinking in the bath. I suspected it was an excuse to justify sitting in a bathtub for an hour. I was willing to conduct my own experiment. Anything for a good cause.

My eyes fluttered open at the sound of paws on the tile floor. "What are you doing in here?"

Raoul held out a paw to reveal a pale pink bath bomb. *It's for stress relief. Thought you might appreciate it.*

I narrowed my eyes. "Where did you get it?"

*Not the dump if that's what you're worried about. I thought you deserved a thank you gift too. It's for stress relief, which you are in desperate need of.*

I debated for half a second. "Fine."

He dropped in the bath bomb and I heard the satisfying hiss as the ball revealed its secrets to the water.

"You can go now. Watching me in the bathtub is a surefire way to increase my stress level."

*10-4, good buddy.* He dropped onto all fours and scampered from the bathroom.

I sank deeper into the water and closed my eyes. At least Florian would be my wingman tonight. He was the ideal companion for an evening like this. Even if his mother found out he was dining with me, all would be forgiven when she heard the name 'Avens-Beech.' They were the kind of coven members she approved of.

Twenty minutes later I climbed out of the bath, feeling more positive in general. Maybe there truly was something to the bath theory. As I toweled off, I noticed red bumps forming on the bare skin of my arms. What in the name of sweet baby Elvis?

I jerked toward the mirror and gasped in horror. My face was covered in the same red bumps.

"Raoul!"

The door cracked open and the raccoon's head poked

through the doorway. *You rang, my liege?* His beady eyes popped at the sight of me. *Ooh. What happened to you?*

I gripped the towel around me. "You happened to me! Where did you get that bath bomb? You said it wasn't from the dump."

*It wasn't.*

"Where. Did. You. Get. It?"

He winced. *I found it by a dumpster in an alley.*

I shrieked. "You said it was for stress relief!"

*Yeah, I smelled lavender. Didn't you?*

The red spots on my skin seemed to grow brighter with each passing second.

*I'm sure it's legit*, he continued. *It was in the alley behind that homemade soap place.*

"These angry red marks tell a different story."

*I'm sure they'll wear off...eventually.*

"I don't have time to wait. Florian will be here in half an hour."

*Use magic or makeup—or magical makeup.*

"I can't believe I trusted you with a basic need like soap. What was I thinking?"

*I'll flip through a spell book while you're getting dressed and see what I can find.*

"You do that." I slammed the door behind him. I'd have to choose a different outfit than the one I'd planned—one that showed the least amount of skin. My face would be the main issue. Because of my dark hair and pale skin, if I wore too much foundation, I risked looking like a ghoul. Magic was my best bet.

By the time I arrived downstairs, clothing on and hair fluffed, Raoul and Marley were elbow-deep in books at the table. Marley glanced up and audibly gulped.

"I know it's bad," I said. "You don't have to hide it."

Marley's shoulders sagged with relief. "Thank goodness because I don't think I could if I wanted to."

"Have you found anything helpful?"

"Not yet."

"You know what? It's fine. I'm not interested in Castor and this will be a surefire way to put him off." I patted Raoul on the head. "You did me a favor."

A horn honked. Florian.

"Bye, Mom. Have fun. Can't wait to meet my new daddy."

"Hardy har. You're hilarious." I hurried from the house before another calamity occurred. I couldn't even blame the ring for this one—or could I?

I laughed when I realized that Castor had chosen Basil for the restaurant. I'd clearly been distracted and only noticed the address when the original text came through. At least I knew I liked the menu and that we wouldn't run into Alec.

Castor and his sister were already at the table when we arrived and the host escorted us directly to them. The wizard had secured the most secluded table in the restaurant. It was actually raised up on a mini-platform in the back corner of the room so that we could observe the entire space from our vantage point.

"Hi, I'm Honey." She extended a hand to each of us. The witch had similar coloring to her brother. Her dark hair was pinned up in an elegant twist and she wore a dress that accentuated her slender build. She was more toned than curvy. It was obvious that exercise was a regular part of her routine.

No one commented on my face, which I thought was incredibly polite. Okay, Florian commented on it in the car. And again in the parking lot. But he was family. It was to be expected.

"In case you're wondering, I don't have the plague. I'm

having some kind of allergic reaction to a bath bomb." I figured I'd get ahead of any speculation.

Over the top of his menu, Castor smiled at me. "I hadn't even noticed."

Liar. But sweet.

"We attended school together," Honey said to Florian. "You probably don't remember though. I wasn't a memorable girl."

"Don't be absurd," Castor said. "You were top of your class."

Florian stared at her, recognition flaring in his eyes. "Dear gods."

"That's right. Avens-Beeched Whale. I think that's what you and your friends called me, isn't it?"

"Actually I think it was Beeched Whale Dipped in Honey," Florian mumbled.

I whacked his arm with my purse. "Florian Rose-Muldoon, are you serious right now?"

"It's fine," Honey said. "I was overweight. They were adolescent boys."

"That doesn't make it acceptable." I could've throttled my cousin on behalf of overweight paranormals everywhere.

"I was a wereass. I'm so sorry."

I'd never seen him so embarrassed. The tips of his ears turned bright red.

Castor closed his menu. "Well, now that we got the introductions out of the way, are we ready to order?"

I laughed.

Honey reached across the table and covered Florian's hands with hers. "It's okay, Florian. Truly. I shouldn't have mentioned it."

"Of course you should have. I'm mortified. I'm not that kid anymore. I promise."

She withdrew her hand. "Glad to hear it. I'm not that girl anymore either. It seems we've both changed."

I was glad we'd cleared that hurdle. I'd brought Florian to feel more comfortable, not less.

Terrence approached the table and immediately recognized me. "Hey, you're back."

Everyone looked at me. "I was here for lunch recently."

"Wanda's working the other section. Sorry you got stuck with me. You did, however, get the best table in the house."

"Glad to hear it," Castor said. "That's always my preference."

We placed our orders and Terrence was back within minutes with a bottle of red wine. I'd been tempted to choose white because of my headaches, but I liked red better. I had painkillers in my purse if necessary.

"So how do you spend your time these days, Florian?" Honey asked.

Florian ran a cloth napkin along his lips. "I log a lot of hours on my boat. I love being on the water."

"What about for work?"

"Oh, I'm on the board of my family's charitable foundation and I work with my sister on the tourism board."

"Honey and I devote time to charities as well," Castor said. "It's so important to give back when we've been so fortunate."

"By sheer luck as well," Honey added. "It's not as though we earned our place in a world of wealth and privilege. We were born into it."

Florian's gaze flicked to me. My cousin wasn't prone to question his good fortune in life and I sensed he felt uncomfortable with their attitude.

"If you haven't read it, I highly recommend *Pearls of Wisdom* by Lavender Moon-Mandrake," Honey said. "It's a wonderful book on philosophy and how it fits in the modern world."

Florian smiled at her. "Sounds great. I'll swing by the library for a copy."

"I'd be happy to lend you mine," Honey said.

I bit the inside of my cheek to keep from laughing. The only time Florian picked up a book was to use it as a coaster and the only time he spent at the library was when he dated Delphine, the town librarian. It was interesting to watch their interactions, though. Florian seemed to be falling all over himself to gain Honey's approval. Castor and I engaged in conversation as well, but it had a perfunctory feel to it, as though Florian and Honey were the real date and we were the wingmen.

*This would be more fun if Granger were here.*

The words hit me so hard and so suddenly that I started to choke. I reached for my glass of water and drank greedily. Florian whacked me between the shoulder blades and went straight back to the conversation about favorite vacation spots.

Talk about left field. Where had that thought come from?

Castor was perfectly charming. His jokes were funny. His smile was endearing. And yet the more we talked, the more I pictured Granger in the seat across from me. The sheriff had a way of improving every situation, even the perfectly pleasant ones like tonight. The realization left me feeling hollow, as though someone had used a melon baller and scooped out my insides. Why now? Why not when I had the chance?

Florian nudged me. "You okay?" he asked under his breath.

I nodded and forced a cheerful smile.

"Tell me more about New Jersey," Castor said. "I find your

history fascinating. Every witch I meet has a similar story, but yours is…" He gazed at me in wonder. "You're like no one I've ever met before."

"I'd be happy to answer that, but first…" I pushed back my chair. "If you'll excuse me, I need the restroom." Castor's attention had grown too intense and I needed a break from it.

"I'll come with you," Honey said, hopping out of her seat.

The restroom was empty except for the attendant. She smiled in recognition when I entered.

"Hi, Kathleen," I said.

"You remember my name?"

"Of course. It wasn't that long ago."

"I know, but…" She shook her head. "Have you found the ring?"

"Not yet. Still working on it."

I ducked into the bathroom and emptied my bladder. Immediate relief.

When I returned to the sink to wash my hands, Honey was already taking a towel from Kathleen to dry hers.

Honey beamed at me. "I have never seen my brother so besotted."

"Yeah, it's weird."

Honey's brow creased. "Why is it weird? You're a smart, beautiful witch with an interesting life."

And I was that same witch when we met at Haverford House, yet he didn't seem particularly keen on me, despite Artemis's prediction. Maybe he'd given it some thought after his meeting with her and decided to give me a chance. That obviously explained arranging the date in the first place, although it seemed more perfunctory then, like he merely wanted to cross me off his list.

"I don't know. He seems different tonight." The longer I sat across from him, the more different he became.

"Because he's crazy for you." She bumped me with her hip. "And your cousin is…very personable."

The attendant fanned herself. "Florian Rose-Muldoon is hotter than the blowtorch they use on the creme brûlée."

"You don't sound enthused," I told Honey. "I know he has a certain reputation, but Florian has many great qualities that have nothing to do with his family name."

Looking at her reflection in the mirror, Honey reapplied her lipstick. "I was worried he'd still be an arrogant wereass, but his manners are impeccable and he seemed genuinely apologetic about our school days."

I smiled. "He can be an ass on occasion, but he can also be sweet and kind. He's wonderful with my daughter. I know he thinks he'd make a terrible dad, but I completely disagree. I think he'll be an amazing one someday."

Honey dropped the tube of lipstick into her purse and snapped it closed. "Thanks, but I'm not sure I want kids. Honestly, I only came as a favor to my brother. I have my career and my family and I'm pretty content with that."

A random guest alighted from a stall and joined us at the row of sinks. "I can't wait to have children. I'd have an entire sports team of my own if I were physically capable of it."

I laughed. "Have one and then see how you feel." As a teen mom, I'd been too young to give motherhood much thought and then I became so overwhelmed with Marley that a second child didn't enter my mind. Then Karl died, of course, and any thought of growing the family went out the window.

I accepted the towel from Kathleen and Honey and I each left a tip in the basket.

"I really hope you'll give my brother a chance," Honey said, as we returned to the table. "If nothing else, it will give us a chance to get to know each other. Good girlfriends are like solid gold in this town. Hard to find but well worth keeping."

I gave her a pointed look. "I'm going to make the same suggestion about Florian."

We took our seats and I was pleased to see dessert had arrived.

"My favorite part of the meal," I said. As I picked up my fork, the manager appeared in the middle of the room. Kevyn's green-tinted brow glittered with tiny beads of sweat. He looked like he belonged in bed with an ice pack and a bowl of chicken broth.

"I must insist that you all leave the premises immediately," Kevyn croaked. He retrieved a handkerchief and dabbed at the moisture that had collected on his forehead. "Don't worry about the bill. We apologize for any inconvenience."

Florian and I exchanged alarmed glances.

"I won't bother to ask if everything's okay," I said.

"Gotta go!" Kevyn rushed to the restroom, prompting a mass exodus. Diners tripped over each other trying to beat a hasty retreat.

Wanda noticed us still seated and approached the table. "He means everyone." Her eyes zeroed in on the fork in my hand. "Please don't eat another bite."

I dropped the fork and the metal clattered against the plate. "What's going on?"

The server leaned forward and lowered her voice. "Health and safety shut us down by emergency order. Apparently the lunch crowd from earlier today is suffering from a bout of food poisoning and they have to investigate."

It seemed that Kevyn was also suffering.

"If they don't know the source, then it could affect the dinner crowd too, right?" Honey asked. Her gaze shifted to her dessert plate. Our table had enjoyed a three-course meal

—well, nearly three courses. I highly doubted dessert was the culprit.

The server waved us along. "Just look out for symptoms. I'm sure someone will be in touch."

My hand moved to rest on my stomach. Terrific. I didn't have room in the schedule to fall ill. Plus, I hated puking. I knew someone in the human world who could drink to excess, puke, and immediately carry on as though nothing had happened, whereas I'd end up in bed for the next twenty-four hours like a corpse with a pulse.

Castor stood and extended a hand toward me. "Shall we?"

I slipped my hand in his. "I think we shall." I was impressed that he didn't seem put off by my appearance. Under the current circumstances, *I* didn't want to touch me, but I had no choice. This wasn't a skin suit I could simply unzip and remove, although that would be both creepy and cool.

"We'll order dessert another time," Castor said, as we exited the building. "That is, if you'd like there to be another time."

I smiled. "Let's wait and see if we emerge from this experience unscathed before we make new plans."

"Fair enough."

Florian stared at Honey in rapt adoration, seemingly in a world of his own. Finally I gripped my cousin by the elbow and steered him to the car.

"Good night," Florian called and blew a kiss at Honey.

"Seriously?" I asked, once we were safely ensconced in the car. "And here I thought you had game."

"She's amazing," he breathed, and started the car. "Don't you think she's amazing?"

"I like her," I admitted. "I just didn't expect you to like her so much. On paper she's a perfect match for you, Florian. If your mother gets wind of it…"

He nodded. "You're right. She'll try to push us together and ruin it. We need to keep this our secret."

I watched a darkened Balefire Beach roll by as we drove past. "Besides, this is you we're talking about. You'll probably lose interest by next week."

"Hey! I resemble that remark."

I glanced over to see him smirk. "I'm surprised you like her. She didn't seem your type."

"Because she's so serious?"

"Delphine was a witch who was into books."

"Delphine is sweet, which I appreciated—or maybe I didn't." He heaved a sigh. "Honey has something else. A spark of intelligence." He frowned. "Not to suggest Delphine isn't smart."

"It's okay. I know what you mean. I take it you intend to ask her out again."

"One hundred percent. I might not even wait my usual three days this time."

Florian seemed to be playing it the opposite of cool. I was curious to see how it worked out. If he'd manage to win Honey over. "It would be great to see you happy with someone."

He looked at me. "Right back at you."

I arrived home feeling exhausted. I opened the door to find Raoul on the sofa and an empty bowl on the coffee table.

"Popcorn?"

He nodded sleepily. *PP3's on Marley's bed. How was your date? Was it true love?*

"Not for me, although he seemed oddly smitten. It was the weirdest thing. When I met him at Haverford House, he seemed perfectly nice, but didn't show much interest in me. Tonight he was like a different guy."

Raoul just stared at me and said, *Huh.*

I eyed him closely. "What did you do?"

He averted his beady eyes. *Nothing.*

I glanced at the red marks on my hands. "That bath bomb wasn't from an alley, was it?"

His silence was deafening.

I moved closer to the sofa and stood in front of him. "Was it?"

*It wasn't for stress relief. I bartered for it.*

"What kind of bath bomb was it?"

*A love bomb.*

I swallowed a scream, not wanting to disturb Marley's sleep. "Why would you do that to me?"

*Because I want you to get over Alec and—let's face it—thanks to your aunt's mishegoss, you could really use a confidence booster.*

My hands rested on my hips. "And you thought a good way to help me with that was to give me the pox?"

*I didn't know you'd have a reaction to it.*

I sank beside him on the sofa. "I appreciate the gesture—really, I do. But it wasn't necessary. I don't want Castor to be in love with me."

*I wasn't sure how it worked. I thought you might like him, or at least be open to the possibility.*

I patted his furry leg. "A part of me will always love Alec, but sometimes love isn't enough and that's okay. I'm not brooding. I'm not hiding from the world."

*I'm sorry. No more magically-infused bath bombs.*

"Will it wear off or do I need to give Castor some kind of antidote?"

Raoul grimaced. *I'm sure I should know the answer.*

I sighed. "But you don't." I rose to my feet. "We'll figure it out tomorrow. I'm going to bed." I started toward the staircase.

*How did it feel?*

I turned to look at him. "How did what feel?"

*How did it feel to have the potential for love again?*

I knew he meant Castor, but my mind was on someone else. I couldn't bring myself to say the words out loud. Not yet. What if the love bomb *had* affected me and that was the result? No. It was best to say nothing.

"Like I said, his behavior seemed out of the blue, but he's a nice wizard. He'll make some witch very happy one day."

But that witch wouldn't be me.

# CHAPTER ELEVEN

I AWOKE the next morning pleased to have avoided food poisoning, although one glimpse in the mirror told me I'd retained the skin irritation from the bath bomb. I showered and dressed before heading downstairs for breakfast. Marley sat at the kitchen table with a spoon in one hand and a book pressed open with the other.

She twisted to look at me. "How was your date?"

"It was a date." I didn't want to explain my complex emotions to my daughter, especially when I didn't quite understand them myself.

"Why are you dressed already? It isn't even noon."

I glared at her. "I don't hang around in pajamas until lunchtime."

"You have ever since you lost your job and broke up with Alec." She returned her focus to the book.

"I'm going back to the restaurant today. They had to close in the middle of the dinner rush last night because of food poisoning."

"Ugh. Good thing you dodged that."

"No kidding."

"Why go back today?"

I poured a cup of coffee. "I'd like more information."

She closed her book and gave me her full attention. "You think it might be the ring?"

I shrugged. "It's possible since that's where the ring was stolen."

"But the engagement party was last week. Why would there be a delay?"

I leaned a hip against the counter and sipped my coffee. "I don't know. That's why I'm going to ask questions. I'd like to rule it out or in."

"Raoul left notes for you. They're hard to understand, but I figured you could decipher raccoon scratches." She pushed a sheet of paper to the edge of the table.

I reviewed the scribbles. Raoul had researched the love bomb, bless his furry, misguided heart. The influence wore off within six to eight hours and there were no lingering effects. Perfect.

Wait. There was nothing about when the spots would disappear. Not so perfect.

I peered out the window to see an unfamiliar car parked outside. PP3 yipped his approval of the visitor. Hmm.

A figured emerged from the car swaddled in a black cloak and with a noticeable hunched back. It was only when she landed on the welcome mat that I realized the cloaked figure was Aster.

"Greeting, old wise woman."

"I come bearing gifts." Aster swept into the cottage and returned to an upright position.

"Is it an apple? If so, I'm going to have to decline because it's clearly been poisoned."

"Mother would never expect me to disguise myself as a decrepit old witch."

"Heaven forbid. What would the neighbors say?"

Aster produced the portfolio that was tucked under her arm and placed it on the dining table. "I'd like to show you the shed options I've drafted for your new office."

I glanced at the clock on my phone. There was still time before anyone would be at the restaurant. "Great. Let's see."

She flipped to the first design, which was in the style of a gingerbread house. There were gables and white trim, as well as a decorative chimney that appeared to be made of colorful candy.

"This one is pretty but not very professional. It looks like I might lure children inside to roast them."

Aster scrutinized the design. "Yes. I can see that." She turned to the next page. "What do you think of this one?"

I cleared my throat, not sure how to respond without sounding rude. "How honest do you want me to be?"

Her gaze flicked to me. "Very. These are prototypes. If you have strong feelings, I'd appreciate hearing them sooner rather than later."

"The outside is fine, but the interior looks like the lair of a serial killer. You'd enter and expect to see soundproof walls and plastic sheets everywhere to contain the blood spatter."

Aster tore the page in half and tapped the next design. "This one?"

The next page showed promise. It was cozy without being too homey. Flower boxes underlined the exterior windows and the inside was reminiscent of a retro campervan with lots of shiny metal and pops of color.

"This one has a lot of potential."

She smiled. "Not too much chintz?"

"Maybe a smidge too much for me, but I like the balance. It's professional yet relaxed." Some offices were too austere and stuffy. If clients were going to bring me their problems and spill their secrets, I wanted them to feel as comfortable as possible.

"I have a few more ideas if you want to see them," Aster said.

"I don't think that's necessary. I'd be happy with something like this."

"Wonderful." She closed the portfolio and hugged it to her chest. "This has been such fun. Every day is a new adventure."

"I'm glad you're enjoying it." Like my father used to say, if you love what you do, you never work a day in your life. "Thanks for doing this, Aster. I know it's not easy sneaking around."

She turned to face me with a determined glint in her eyes. "Our family has endured worse. We'll get through this."

"Next time you speak to Florian, ask him about our double date last night."

She puckered her lips. "Ooh, do tell."

"He may have developed quite the crush on one Honey Avens-Beech." Assuming it wasn't the influence of the love bomb.

She frowned. "Avens-Beech? But they're a respectable coven family. Why would he be interested in her?"

"I know, right? How unlike him. Apparently he was cruel to her at the academy as well, but she seems cool about it now."

"We can't tell Mother. She'll be booking the venue and hiring the caterers."

"I know. There's a bigger problem though. I'm not so sure Honey is interested."

"Is she straight?"

"Yes. She just sees Florian the way a lot of residents do. Handsome and charming but feckless."

Aster tapped her sculpted fingernails on the table. "Then I suppose he'll have to prove her wrong."

"Let's leave this up to him. We can't do his dating for him too. This is how he ended up being Florian in the first place."

"True. I can't wait to tell Linnea. She'll be so excited."

"Please don't tell anyone else. I don't want your mother to get wind of it too soon."

Aster pretended to zip her lip. She hurried from the cottage, careful to hunch over once she crossed the threshold.

---

The first thing I noticed when I arrived at Basil was Sheriff Nash's patrol car parked out front. It seemed the sheriff was conducting a little investigation of his own.

I entered the restaurant and spotted him at the back of the room, deep in conversation with an unfamiliar elf. Based on Kevyn's appearance last night, I didn't expect to see him today.

I gave an awkward wave. "Hi. I hate to interrupt."

The sheriff pivoted toward me and frowned. "Hey, Rose. What are you doing here?"

I could pinpoint the exact moment he noticed my red spots. "I was here last night when they closed. I was hoping to get more information."

All the color had drained from the elf's face. "My heartfelt apology, ma'am. Nothing like this has ever happened to us before. We're trying to get to the bottom of it."

"You haven't identified the source yet?" I asked.

The elf shook his head. "This is a PR nightmare. It could ruin us."

"Would it be possible to see a list of everyone who dined here yesterday?" I asked.

"Lunch and dinner?" the elf asked.

"Just lunch." Whatever happened, it was during the afternoon.

"One moment, please." He darted to the office.

"Is this the ring or a coincidence?" Sheriff Nash asked.

"That's what I'm trying to decide."

It felt strange to be standing in the same restaurant as last night when I had the thought about wishing he were here. And now he was.

The elf returned with a printed sheet of names. I scanned the list and one jumped out at me. I handed the list back to him. "Thanks."

The sheriff intercepted the sheet of paper. "I'll take that for now."

"You really think this might be a criminal act?" the elf asked.

"Not necessarily, but the more information we have, the better." The sheriff folded the paper into a square and tucked it in his pocket.

I hadn't made it to my car when the sheriff fell in step beside me. "You were eating here last night?"

"Yes. Everything was delicious right up until they closed."

"You and Marley?"

"Me and Florian." I paused. "And Castor and Honey Avens-Beech."

"Are they married?"

"Brother and sister."

His brow lifted. "A double date with Florian? What would Hyacinth say?"

"Florian is an adult who makes his own decisions."

He chuckled. "We both know that's not strictly true."

"This is where the ring was stolen, by the way," I told him.

He glanced over his shoulder at the restaurant. "A food poisoning outbreak is definitely bad luck."

"And the owner can't identify the source of the poisoning. He had to close down his business."

The sheriff scratched the nape of his neck. "It's not good."

He made a noise at the back of his throat. "I hate to ask because it's none of my business…"

"Yes, it was a date. No, I didn't like him. I mean, I liked him but not in that way."

He bit back a smile. "I was only going to ask about your skin there. Do you think that's because of the ring too?"

Embarrassment colored my cheeks. "No. This is Raoul's handiwork. It should clear up any day now." I declined to offer any further details.

"Which name?" he asked.

I squinted at him. "Excuse me?"

"Which name did you recognize on the list? I know you, Rose. Your eyes do this little twitchy thing when you know something." He pointed to the corner of his eye, drawing my attention to their dark depths. Whereas Alec's eyes had been an icy blue that gave nothing away, Granger's brown eyes radiated warmth and compassion.

I snapped back to reality. "My client's half-brother. He was here yesterday."

"Ah. Have you already spoken to him about the ring?"

"No. Ben didn't think he was a suspect."

"A half-brother? That's surprising. Why not?"

"Because there are two likely reasons the ring was stolen—to sell for money or to attract love. Tyler has money and he isn't interested in love. He's basically the Florian of their family."

The sheriff chuckled again. "I guess you're going to have to add him to your list."

"As a matter of fact, he's my next stop." He stared at me for a beat too long and I rubbed my cheek self-consciously. "What? I told you these spots will clear up soon."

His mouth twitched in amusement. "It isn't that. I was just thinking how pretty you look today."

"Cut it out. I saw the second your brain registered these beauty marks."

"I think you know me well enough by now to know I don't really notice the superficial stuff, Rose. I just see you." He turned and sauntered to his car without another word, whistling as he walked.

I ducked behind the wheel and tried to calm the beating of my heart. Last night I'd asked myself why now. If Florian could mature later in life, why not me? Granted, I was a mother and probably should've sorted out my emotional self long before now, but that didn't mean it was too late. I'd been working on myself for months, which was the reason I ended my relationship with Alec.

The age of eighteen made me a legal adult, but it didn't mean I had everything figured out by then. I'd been forced to become an adult before I was ready. My mom's early death. Marley's birth. My dad and Karl. I'd gone through a lot and spent my energy on survival and not much else. Only in Starry Hollow when the stress of survival had eased did I finally get the chance to focus on my internal needs. And my inner child had chosen Alec. Funny thing about children—they're not the best decision makers. So who was I now? Whose needs was I trying to meet?

I started the engine and turned up the soothing sound of Springsteen.

As hard as it was, I was growing up.

# CHAPTER TWELVE

According to Tyler's social media posts, of which there were many, I could find him at the local boxing center.

The interior space was enormous. There were several rings, as well as an area that housed weights and punching bags.

"Well, well, well. If you're up for a little action, I wouldn't mind sparring with you, although my brother might not approve."

I didn't need to turn around to know that Wyatt Nash was behind me. "Don't think your ex-wife would approve either." Wyatt twice in one week? The ring was definitely to blame.

He chuckled. "Nothing new there. Linnea doesn't approve of anything I do." His gaze raked over me. "You don't look dressed for a match. What are you doing here?"

"Looking for a shifter named Tyler. Do you know him?"

Wyatt angled his head toward the center ring. "I see him here three days a week, which means he's probably here at least five."

"Can you tell me anything about him?"

Wyatt smirked. "Why? Thinking about embarking on a new relationship?" He shook his head. "Poor Granger. You'll crush his bleeding heart all over again."

"I'm here for work."

"Right. And I'm here for the smoothies." He paused. "Actually the smoothies are delicious. I highly recommend the burstberry."

"I'm not here for a smoothie but thanks."

"I know we give each other a hard time, but I think it's awesome that you're taking a stand with your aunt. I knew you had guts. One of my issues with Linnea was that she cares too much what her mother thinks."

"She married you, didn't she?"

"I know, but Hyacinth…You know how she is. That disapproval put a strain on the marriage."

"I'd say running around with other women put more of a strain on it."

Wyatt wagged a finger at me. "I can see why you're so appealing to my brother. He likes a woman who can hold her own…" His lips melted into a lazy grin. "…and his."

Inwardly I groaned. "It's been a joy talking to you, but I have work to do."

He winked. "You mean Tyler to do."

Before I could object, he tossed a towel over his shoulder and sauntered away. It still amazed me that Granger and Wyatt were related and grew up in the same household. The brothers were like a family experiment gone awry.

There were two shifters sparring in the center ring, one older and one younger. Despite the age gap, it was clear the older shifter had years of experience. There was a certain grace to his movements that seemed in direct contrast to his muscular body. Although I didn't know much about boxing, Tyler's practiced movements were to the point of unnatural, whereas his opponent moved as though born with boxing gloves on his hands. Neither shifter seemed aware of my presence. That was fine. I found myself mesmerized by their match. I could tell a lot about someone by the way they played a sport and boxing was no exception. Tyler was all flash and no substance, which was exactly what I would've expected of him based on what I knew. His movements were designed not to win, but to impress. His opponent took advantage of Tyler's strutting and posturing and knocked him backwards. The werecheetah landed flat on his back and brushed off the older shifter when he offered a hand to help him to his feet.

"Nice moves," I said.

"Thanks," Tyler said.

I smiled. "I was talking to him." I angled my head toward his opponent.

The older shifter grinned. "Finally. A woman with taste."

Tyler waved me forward. "Are you here to learn? Because I'd be more than happy to teach you a few of my best moves."

I leaned against the ropes. "I'm pretty sure I've just seen them and I'll pass."

The older shifter chuckled. "Looks like you're getting beaten physically and verbally today, Ty."

Tyler noticed my skin and grimaced. "What happened to your face?"

"I was at a furry convention and I wore my gorilla mask a little too long."

His upper lip curled slightly as he gazed at me with uncertainty. "How can I help you?"

I stuck out a hand. "I'm Ember Rose. I work for Ben."

Reluctantly Tyler shook my hand. "My brother? What does he have you doing?"

"I'm investigating the stolen engagement ring."

Confusion marred his attractive features. "Engagement ring? You mean Nanny's ring he gave to Lindsey?"

"That's right. It was stolen the night of the engagement party. You didn't hear?"

"That ring has been collecting dust in the family vault for decades," Tyler said. "It's been out for what—a whole two weeks—and now it's gone? I knew it was a bad idea for Nanny to let them have it."

"You didn't agree with letting Ben have the ring?"

"No, as a matter of fact I didn't, and I told Nanny as much."

"What did she say when you expressed your concern?"

He gave a rueful shake of his head. "Nanny hasn't been herself lately. I think her age is finally catching up with her. I'm the oldest grandson. She's always listened to me, but I couldn't seem to get her to listen to reason this time." He banged his gloved hands on the top rope. "And now it's gone. Great."

"What would you have preferred Nanny do with the ring? You said yourself it's been collecting dust in a vault."

"I know, but at least nobody could steal it from there. If the ring was stolen from a public place, it could be anywhere by now. We'll never get it back."

"Except the restaurant wasn't open to the public for the engagement party," I pointed out. "The guests were limited to invited family members and close friends."

"Well, I don't need the money. If I were you, I'd be looking at staff. We had to fire a few cleaners when I was a kid. One even stole a bike out of the garage. Can you believe it?"

"Money isn't the only reason to steal the ring. It could be someone who didn't want the ring to leave the family."

He scoffed. "That's ridiculous. Lindsey will be family as soon as they're married and even if the wedding fell through for some reason, she's the kind of paranormal who would give the ring back. She's a good girl. She'd never keep another family's heirloom."

"Why did you leave the party early?" I asked. It made sense that if he was the thief, he would exit as quickly as possible.

"I had a date, but I wasn't permitted to bring a guest to the party, so I arranged to meet her after." The corners of his mouth tugged. "Madison was a far better dessert than anything on the menu there."

Lovely. "Maybe leaving early was part of your plan. You knew you were going to take the ring and so you set up the date as an alibi."

He grunted. "Sure, I want to keep the ring in the family, but I have no interest in keeping it for myself. I'm never getting married and I have plenty of money. What other motive is there?"

"It doesn't have to be a rational one," I said. "If you didn't think Ben should have the ring, that's motive enough to steal it back."

"And then what? It's not like my family would forget about it. What would I do with it? I couldn't sell it because that would defeat the purpose of keeping it in the family. I'd be stuck hiding a valuable piece of jewelry for the rest of my life." He shook his head. "No thanks. I don't need that kind of pressure."

"I understand you were back at the same restaurant for lunch yesterday. Did you recognize anyone there? Any relatives?" It was possible someone had been there as a guest and wasn't on the owner's list of paying customers.

Tyler appeared thoughtful. "No. I met a friend there, though, and the poor dude's in rough shape. I was glad I didn't order the shrimp."

"What happened?" the older shifter asked.

"Food poisoning," Tyler said. "Artie's in the hospital. His girlfriend texted me last night to make sure I was okay."

"There was an outbreak. They haven't identified the source yet." Although I had a strong inclination the source wasn't food-based.

Tyler jabbed at the air. "If I were you, I'd talk to that cousin of Lindsey's."

"Which one?"

"The bridezilla. Hot as anything, but major attitude problems." He banged his thick gloves together. "Kayla. That's her name. I feel sorry for that poor sap who's going to be stuck with her for the rest of his life. A difficult bride is a difficult wife."

The older shifter gave his arm a playful tap. "Like you would know anything about a wife."

"What makes you suspect Kayla other than the fact that she's…difficult?"

"She was at my table, which is one of the reasons I was thrilled to escape early. She would not shut up about the fact that Ben and Lindsey's wedding is only a few weeks before hers. Every comment was a gripe. If you look up 'bitter bride,' there's a picture of Kayla with her arms crossed."

"Thanks for the tip." Interesting that Ben didn't seem to suspect Kayla. On the other hand, he'd been focused on members of his own family when he wrote his list of suspects. He didn't include any of Lindsey's.

I turned to go.

"Rushing off so soon?" Tyler called. "Come on. Don't be shy. I'll show you a few moves. I'm an excellent teacher."

"I have a lot of work to do."

"Just one quick round."

Tyler was my least favorite type of guy—one who wasn't willing to take no for an answer. I climbed into the ring and let the older shifter fit me with gloves.

"Don't worry," Tyler cooed. "I'll go easy on you." He paused, his lips curving into a salacious smile. "Unless you like it rough."

I banged my gloves together and winked. "I'm game. Let's see what you can do to me."

Tyler seemed to like that invitation. "Don't worry, babe. My touch is very gentle. Ask any of the women I've tangled with."

I danced around the ring like I'd seen Sylvester Stallone do in the Rocky movies. You didn't grow up in the shadow of Philadelphia without making at least one iconic run up the many steps of the art museum and celebrating your success at the top.

"Keep grooving, dancing queen," he said, visibly irritated. "A moving target is still a target."

I moonwalked across the ring, maintaining a nonchalant demeanor. The less I seemed to care, the more aggravated Tyler was.

"Are we boxing or having a dance contest? This is why I don't fight girls."

"I thought you were an excellent teacher," I shot back. "Where's the lesson?"

"I'll show you the lesson." He cut straight across the ring, swinging wide.

I scooped as much magic as I could into a single concentrated ball. I didn't just go full descendant of the One True Witch. I went full Jersey too. Tyler never stood a chance.

"*Pulso*," I said. As my glove connected with his chest, I released the ball of magic.

Tyler flew backward like an entire row of linebackers charged him at once. He slammed against the ropes and bounced twice before dropping face down on the floor of the ring.

The older shifter hooted with delight. "Man, if I had

known it was going to go down like that, I would've recorded it. I'd pay good money to watch that again."

I clapped my gloves together. "I'm willing."

"Not me. I have better things to do." Tyler struggled to his feet. "Time to hit the showers." He ripped off the gloves and tossed them to the floor. "And no, you're not invited. Your loss."

I swallowed a laugh. "Maybe next time, Tyler."

# CHAPTER THIRTEEN

I MANAGED to track down Kayla at a bridal gown shop on Sparkle Row. The entire street seemed dedicated to dresses for special occasions much like Seers Row was dedicated to fortune tellers.

The plump fairy behind the counter fluttered over to greet me with a wide smile. Her wings were covered in multicolored rhinestones.

"Welcome. I'm Debbie. And who do we have with us today? Bride, bridesmaid, or wedding guest?"

She spoke to me as though I were a kindergartner who needed to know which art supplies were available for use.

"Actually I'm here for Kayla." I left my answer deliberately vague. I didn't actually say I was a friend, so it wasn't a lie.

Debbie clapped her hands. "You came at the right time. Kayla has just put on her wedding gown. It's her second fitting so I'm sure it will be perfect this time."

She guided me to a back room that was nearly the same size as the showroom. It was set up like a fancy dressing room with plush jewel-toned sofas, a raised platform, and the kind of soft lighting that made every face appear camera-ready. The entire room was encircled by mirrors, presumably so the bride could see how she looked to others from every possible angle. It seemed like overkill to me. Then again, I'd probably buy a dress off the rack in the sale section and call it a day.

Kayla stood on the raised platform in a pale pink dress. Her blond hair was pulled into a messy bun and she was examining the train in the mirror behind her. The strapless bodice was made of tiny beads that sparkled even in the dim lighting.

"This train is too short," Kayla whined.

The seamstress stood on the floor just below the steps of the platform. "I altered it according to your specifications, miss."

"You most certainly did not. If you had, then I wouldn't be looking at a train that's too short."

"Kayla, sweetie, you did ask them to shorten the train." I had no doubt the woman speaking was Kayla's mother. She was an older carbon copy of the displeased bride.

Kayla spun toward her mother with her hands pressed against her puffy hips. "You promised me this wedding would be perfect. If this train is too short, then it's not perfect, is it?"

If Kayla stomped her foot and demanded an Oompa Loompa next, it wouldn't have surprised me in the least.

"Excuse me, Miss Bevins," the fairy interrupted. "I hate to interrupt, but your friend is here to see you." The fairy backed out of the room, seemingly afraid to be Kayla's next target.

Kayla pinned her gaze on me and scowled. "I don't know you."

"No, sorry. I was hoping to speak to you about a delicate matter. Would it be possible to clear the room for a minute?"

"You heard the lady. Everybody out," Kayla demanded.

I hadn't expected it to be that easy. The seamstress didn't have to be told twice. She rushed past me, her elbow clipping me on the way out. Kayla's mother walked at a slower pace, but her expression was also one of relief.

Kayla turned to face her reflection. "I owe you one. I was ready to scream bloody murder. I feel like I haven't had a moment of peace since we announced our engagement. I can only imagine how actual royals feel."

At least she seemed less hostile now that the others had fled.

"It's a pretty dress," I said. "I've never seen a pink bridal gown before."

"I've always wanted pale pink, like the color of a fading sunset." Kayla's fingers toyed with the full skirt. "I've been planning this wedding since I was six years old. Of course, back then I was going to marry Samuel Stone. He was the cutest boy in my class. Last I heard he works as a night janitor in a high school. Guess I dodged a bullet there."

More like *he* dodged one. "I can see you're busy, so I'll get to the point. I've been hired by Ben to find the missing engagement ring."

Her face flickered with annoyance. "I can't catch a break, can I? Even at my own dress fitting, I have to hear about Lindsey's stupid wedding." She jerked her attention back to her reflection.

"Well, I imagine Lindsey would be upset for you if it had been your engagement ring that was stolen."

Kayla barked a laugh. "Please. Lindsey doesn't think about anyone but herself. I mean, how rude is it to wear an engagement ring like hers when she knows how much bigger it is than mine?"

I stared at her. "Lindsey didn't choose her engagement ring. It's a family heirloom that belonged to Ben's grandmother."

"Oh, I understand that, but if they're going to make the decision to hold their wedding within weeks of mine, which was already on everyone's calendars, then she should at least have the decency to not show off her bling."

"I see. So you had chosen your date and then Ben and Lindsey planned their wedding within weeks of yours?"

She fidgeted with her bodice, hiking it up to cover the tops of her breasts. "Not only did she get engaged after me, but then she had the wherewithal to have her wedding before mine. We had already chosen our venue and set the date. She could've at least waited six months. Now everyone will compare our wedding to hers just like they were comparing my engagement ring to hers." She held up her hand that sported a beautiful pink diamond.

"Your ring is gorgeous, Kayla," I said. Karl hadn't been in a position to afford an engagement ring when we got married, not that I minded. I wasn't much of a jewelry person anyway. I certainly had no interest in being the belle of the ball like Kayla clearly did.

"My ring looks like a pea next to her cantaloupe of a rock. Serves her right for flaunting it in public."

Kayla's bitterness seeped out of her pores. I'd heard of bridezillas, of course, but this was my first direct experience with one.

"Can you believe they even chose the same wedding song?" she huffed. "And because their wedding is first, everyone will think I copied off her, as if that would ever happen. Lindsey isn't capable of an original idea. I swear the only reason she agreed to marry Ben is because I was already engaged."

That seemed highly unlikely. From my vantage point, Lindsey seemed to have a good head on her shoulders, and she and Ben seemed happy together.

She hiked up the bottom half of her dress and scrutinized

her ankles in the mirrors from various angles. "If you want to accuse somebody of stealing the ring, talk to Fatima."

"Who's Fatima?" Another name not on Ben's list.

"Lindsey's former sister-in-law."

"She was at the engagement party?"

"Oh, sure. She and Lindsey stayed real friendly because heaven forfend Lindsey upset anyone." Kayla rolled her eyes.

"If they're friendly, why do you think Fatima might've stolen the ring?"

"Because Lindsey's brother owes a mountain of child support and Fatima is just the type to take matters into her own hands." Kayla dropped her voice to a whisper. "She's not one of us. I'm sure that's half the reason the marriage failed."

"What do you mean? She's human?"

Kayla blew a raspberry. "Heck no. That marriage never would've gotten off the ground. I mean she's not a shifter."

"What is she?"

"A siren. The family thinks she lured Greg into marrying her using her magic."

"If she could lure him into marriage using her magic, then surely she can lure him into paying child support without the need to resort to theft," I pointed out.

Kayla dropped the hem of her dress to the floor. "I'm only repeating what's been said."

"Why doesn't her ex-husband pay child support?"

Kayla shrugged. "He's a cheap wereass. I hope Lindsey doesn't expect a nice wedding gift from her brother. It wouldn't surprise me if he gave her an envelope full of coupons."

I snorted. "Any idea where I can find her?"

"She works at the aquarium."

"Thanks." I paused. "I know it's none of my business, but have you talked to Lindsey about how you feel?" Not that I was here to play family therapist.

She wrinkled her nose. "You mean, like, actually tell her I'm angry?"

"Yes."

"Why would I do that? It's much easier to complain behind her back."

"I know, but it doesn't resolve anything. The problem festers until it explodes and the next thing you know, you and Lindsey aren't on speaking terms and family members are showing up at your house using illusion spells so they don't get in trouble for choosing sides."

Kayla popped her lips. "Um, I think you might be prospecting."

"Projecting?"

She flicked a dismissive finger. "Whatever."

"I'm serious, Kayla. If this wedding business upsets you as much as it seems to, you should clear the air."

"That serves no purpose. Neither one of us will budge on the wedding date. You know what they say—most feelings are best left buried."

I frowned. "What? Nobody says that. Feelings are best expressed."

"So whatever feelings you have about family members—you've expressed them?"

"More or less." Okay, maybe less, but I haven't remained silent on the subject.

Kayla assessed me. "I'm only getting married this once… Well, twice if he dies first. I refuse to be alone for the rest of my life, but he knows that." She lifted her chin. "I was very upfront about it."

"I'm sure he was relieved to know you'd be able to carry on in the event of his untimely death."

She narrowed her eyes. "You're mocking me."

"No." I paused. "Maybe a little. You're not wrong though."

"What do you mean?"

"My husband died young. I think he would've liked to know that I'd be okay." We didn't have that luxury though, not when the death was sudden and unexpected.

Kayla's expression softened. "And are you?" She glanced at my hand. "You didn't remarry."

"My life's been complicated since then."

Kayla stepped down from her pedestal and engulfed me in a hug. The moment of compassion took me off guard.

"It's okay," she said, patting my back like she was burping a baby. "With a little more makeup and a couple less pounds, I'm sure you'll meet someone."

My jaw set. "Fewer," I said through clenched teeth.

"Sorry?"

I disentangled myself from her embrace. "Fewer pounds."

Kayla offered a sympathetic smile. "Exactly."

## CHAPTER FOURTEEN

The aquarium was a staple of the Starry Hollow seaside, not far from the broomstick tours. Marley and I had visited on multiple occasions, although we hadn't returned since the time she cried in front of the shark tank because she decided it was wrong to keep them in captivity for our amusement. We'd discussed it on the way home and I understood her point of view. I also understood that places like aquariums helped educate us and fostered a healthy interest in marine life that might not exist otherwise. Even now I wasn't sure where I stood on the subject.

I approached the ticket counter where two elves were arguing over whether recycling was better or worse for the environment. Marley would've fit right in here.

"Hi," I interrupted. "I'm looking for Fatima."

The elf on the left hooked a thumb over his shoulder. "She's giving a tour to one of our primary school classes. They're probably near the crustacean tank by now."

"Yum," I replied.

He gave me a look of disapproval. No lobster jokes. Got it.

"If you want to go in, you need a ticket," the second elf said.

"I'm not here for the exhibits. I only want to speak to Fatima for five minutes."

"Then you can wait for her in the parking lot," the first elf said. "Otherwise you need to buy a ticket."

Fine. It was for a worthy cause since part of the proceeds were allocated to marine life organizations. I paid and the first elf handed me a ticket which the second elf immediately took.

"Seems like a waste of paper," I remarked. "Might want to think about that next time you're debating how to save the environment."

I sauntered past them and hustled along the long corridor, trying not to get distracted by the colorful tanks. I loved a pretty fish as much as the next paranormal, but I had other priorities.

It was easy to catch up to the group of primary school children. They likely wanted to stop and admire each and every creature along the way. A dark-haired woman stood at the head of the surprisingly orderly line. She was average height with broad shoulders and umber skin that seemed dusted with flecks of gold. Her hair fell past her shoulders, the sides clipped together at the back. She wore a blue collared shirt tucked into a denim skirt, which seemed to be the aquarium uniform.

Excited murmurs escaped the children and I realized they were in front of the shark tank. Now I understood why they hadn't progressed as far as the crustacean tank. The children were mesmerized by the enormous tank with its variety of eels, fish, and, of course, sharks. As long as one of them didn't break down and cry or protest their captivity, I'd be able to eke a few minutes out of Fatima.

I went to the head of the line and stood on the other side of her. "Are you Fatima?"

She looked at me sideways with a pleasant expression. "Yes. Are you from the newspaper?"

My heart jumped. "The newspaper?" Did she somehow recognize me from *Vox Populi*?

"Yes. They said they were sending someone over today to write an article about the new enclosure."

My stomach unclenched. I wasn't sure why the mention of the newspaper rattled me.

Actually that was a lie. I knew exactly why it rattled me. It reminded me of a life I was no longer living and it hurt.

"No, not the newspaper. I'm here on behalf of a client." I didn't want to mention the stolen ring within earshot of the children. "Can I just have a few minutes of your time?" I started toward the far wall and she followed me.

"What's this about? Who's your client?" She looked me up and down. "You don't look like a lawyer."

"I'm not a lawyer." Although I was mildly offended not to look like one. I glanced down at my Witches Be Crazy T-shirt and shredded jeans. Maybe I needed to start wearing a suit to appear more professional. "I'm here to talk to you about a missing ring."

"Fight! Fight!" the kids began to chant.

I glanced at the main tank to see two sharks attacking each other.

"Excuse me for a moment." Fatima hurried over to the tank and faced the sharks. She opened her arms and started to sing.

I didn't understand a single word, but the sounds she produced were haunting. The sharks slowed their movements until finally they broke apart and swam to opposite corners of the tank.

One of the larger kids scowled at her. "Boo." He gave her a thumbs down.

She ruffled his hair. "Sorry, Timothy. No blood in the water today." She turned back to me and shrugged. "Vampire," she said, in a tone that suggested 'what can you do?' "Sorry, you were saying something about a missing ring?"

"I understand you recently attended Ben and Lindsey's engagement party."

Her thick eyebrows drew together. "That's right."

"Were you surprised to be invited?"

"Of course not. Lindsey's still family, no matter how her wereass of a brother behaves."

"I'm surprised you wanted to attend. Sounds like it would be difficult being in the same room with him."

A peal of laughter escaped her full lips. Even her laugh had a musical quality.

"He's the one who was uncomfortable sharing oxygen with me and I have no problem with that." Her face hardened. "He deserves every moment of discomfort."

"Why is that?"

She shifted her gaze to the children to make sure they were occupied before returning her attention to me.

"He hasn't paid child support in a full year. Two kids who are growing by the day and involved in all manner of activities."

And I couldn't imagine a job at the aquarium kept her flush with cash. "I assume you've taken him to court."

She grunted. "What a scam. He just lies about his income and they lower his payments to make it more manageable for him." She used air quotes around 'manageable.'

"But he still doesn't pay?"

Her eyes hardened into two dark stones. "Nope. And to add salt to the wound, he's been on vacation with his new girlfriend and even bought her a new car."

Yikes. No wonder Fatima wanted to make him squirm. She was right—he deserved every uncomfortable moment.

"Have you spoken to his family to see if they can put pressure on him?"

"I've tried. They've tried." Her shoulders sagged. "This is what happens when parents treat their sons like they walk on water. They start to believe the hype and do whatever they want."

"Have any members of his family offered financial support?"

Fatima pressed her lips together. "I'd love to say yes. I know it's not their responsibility—it's totally his—but I would've appreciated even a small token. Georgie's feet seem to grow another half size each month. Do you have any idea how much shoes for kids cost? Plus all the special shoes for sports."

"Have you asked the family for help directly?"

She met my inquisitive gaze. "Would *you*?"

"Greg thinks I should get a job that pays more, like that's the right resolution to this issue."

Two of the boys began climbing on top of the back of a bench and jumping to the floor.

"Clive! Stu! No more of that, please." Fatima's melodic voice filled the air and the boys immediately complied. They slid their butts on the bench and stayed put.

"Wow. Do your own kids ever misbehave?"

"Of course. They're children, but I admit it's easier for me to keep them in line." Her lips curved into a satisfied smile. "So why are you asking me these questions? I get the feeling you're not here about child support."

"Not directly." Although Fatima didn't seem like she'd resort to theft to get the money she was owed, I had to ask. "Lindsey's engagement ring was stolen during the party."

I let the semi-accusation hang in the air between us. It took a minute for the words to register.

As I expected, Fatima appeared affronted, splaying a hand on her chest in a protest of innocence. "And you think I stole it in lieu of payments owed?"

"I don't think anything. I'm just here to ask the question. Given your situation with Lindsey's brother, it's not out of the realm of possibility."

She snorted. "I saw that ring. If I'd stolen it for money, I'd have quit my job to stay home with my kids full-time."

"But that would've drawn attention to you. Maybe you've got it socked away somewhere, biding your time and waiting for the right moment to offload it."

She cocked her head and looked me directly in the eye. "Do you really think that?"

"No," I admitted. "But I wouldn't be doing my job if I didn't follow every lead."

Her mouth turned down at the corners. "Did Lindsey ask you to talk to me? Does she suspect me?"

"Not at all," I said quickly. "In fact, you weren't on the original list, but your name came up during an interview."

She nodded. "Makes sense. I can see why you felt this was necessary, but I had nothing to do with stealing the ring. I adore Lindsey. I would never do anything to cause her pain."

I believed her.

She clasped my hand. "Will you tell Lindsey I had nothing to do with it? I'd hate for her to think for one second that I'd stoop so low. I'm a fierce advocate for my kids, but there are lines I would never cross."

I squeezed her hand and let go. "I'll tell her."

Fatima clapped her hands and sang, "Line up! Everybody line up."

For a brief moment, I was whisked back to Marley's childhood and the recess song from *Bubble Guppies*. Of course, the siren's version was less energetic and more soothing.

"Good luck with your child support case," I said. Despite my improved situation, I remembered how it felt to be a single mom with limited resources.

It was hard.

I walked past the obedient line of children and exited the aquarium. Although I was disappointed to have struck out again, I was relieved to rule out Fatima. Part of me wanted to interrogate Greg for the fun of it, but the priority was finding the ring before all hell broke loose.

And I knew just where to go next.

# CHAPTER FIFTEEN

Now that I'd ruled out Tyler, Kayla, and Fatima, I drove straight to the hospital to speak to Tyler's friend, Artie, as well any other food poisoning victims. It was possible one of them had noticed someone wearing the aquamarine ring.

The moment I arrived at the entrance, I knew something was wrong. Several members of the Silver Moon coven hovered in the lobby and Deputy Bolan was issuing orders to hospital personnel.

I joined Iris Sandstone by the reception desk. Iris was the Head Priestess of our coven and would likely have the answers to my burning questions.

"What's going on?"

Iris cast a sidelong glance at me. "The hospital lost power earlier and the backup generator isn't working. They've requested magical assistance."

Oh, wow. No wonder everyone looked so tense. Patients could die.

"Is there anything I can do to help?"

"We're awaiting instructions, but I'm sure your magic would be most welcome."

Deputy Bolan broke away from his conversation and scurried over to the gathering of witches and wizards. His gaze fell on me and, for once, he didn't scowl.

"Perfect timing. We can use your help, Rose."

If the situation weren't so dire, I would've asked him to say it again for posterity. "I'll do whatever I can."

"According to the hospital administrator, the second floor is the most critical," the deputy said.

"On it," I said.

Iris addressed the rest of the group. "We'll work here in the lobby and try to get power flowing to the rest of the building." She turned to the leprechaun. "If you could clear the area of all non-essential workers, that would be helpful."

Deputy Bolan didn't hesitate. A shrill whistle erupted from his lips and he began issuing orders.

I rushed to the stairwell and headed to the second floor where I nearly collided with a nurse.

"I'm so sorry." Her arms were laden with thick blankets. "I'm afraid visiting hours have been cancelled until further notice."

"I'm a witch. I'm going to try and get this floor up and running."

The nurse blew out a relieved breath. "Thank the gods. Nothing like this has ever happened before. It's the whole point of a backup generator."

It seemed like the Ring of Despair had found its way to the hospital. It was possible the thief had been here to visit Nanny before she died and bad luck had taken root, although that seemed too far removed in time. The more likely scenario was that whoever had the ring at the restaurant ended up here with food poisoning. Like an infectious disease, the ring's influence was spreading. I had to find it before the entire town was infected by it. Ben's grandmother had been wrong to store it in a vault all these years. She should have destroyed it.

The nurse directed me to the central station where staff members were collecting blankets, bottles of water, and other necessities for their patients.

"Clear the way," the nurse called. "Witch in residence."

I shot off an urgent text to Marley and explained the situation. She should be home from school by now, which meant she'd be able to act as the Willow to my Buffy.

*BRB*, she replied, which I now understood meant 'be right back' rather than 'buy roast beef.' The urban dictionary had saved me from making a complete fool of myself on multiple occasions.

I felt dozens of eyes on me as I awaited a response from Marley. I lowered the phone and offered them a reassuring smile.

"Excuse me, ma'am," a nurse called. "We've asked all visitors to evacuate the building."

I glanced over my shoulder to see Wanda, the server from Basil, lingering in a doorway. Had she been struck down by food poisoning or was she checking on her customers?

"I told her she could stay with her son," another nurse whispered. "He's only six and he got really scared when everything turned off."

Her son was here?

"So did I," a third nurse said. "I kinda wish my mom was here too."

Wanda crossed the corridor and her face lit up in recognition at the sight of me. "You're a Rose, right? Are you here to help?"

I nodded. "Someone mentioned you're here with your son. I assume it isn't food poisoning."

"Oh, no. He's been sick."

I suddenly remembered her checking on her son when

she waited on me. "He came home from school sick the day I met you."

Her expression clouded over. "That's right. He got much worse and I ended up bringing him here. They think it's an autoimmune disease, but they're still running tests because they can't figure it out. He seems to get weaker by the day."

A horrible thought occurred to me. What if this poor woman's son was critically ill because of the ring? The ring's presence at the restaurant seemed to spark a series of unfortunate events that threatened to continue unless I could find it. I felt a surge of panic. Wanda was a single mom like me, although it sounded like the dad was involved. I didn't have that luxury. What if something bad happened to me? What would happen to Marley? Would Aunt Hyacinth take advantage of the opportunity to swoop in and mold Marley in her image? I pushed aside my fears. Now wasn't the time.

My phone pinged with an incoming text. Marley. I scanned the long message and made sure I understood the spell before I attempted it. With the way things were going, I didn't want to risk a misunderstanding.

"Does anyone have chalk?" I asked.

Wanda held up a finger. "I do!" She started to root through her bag. "Does it matter if it isn't white? I usually carry a pack in my purse because my son likes to draw on the sidewalk with it, but I only have green, pink, and blue."

"Any color is fine."

She produced a broken piece of pale green chalk and handed it to me. I drew a circle around me on the linoleum floor and sat cross-legged in the middle of it.

"Is that supposed to be a circle?" one of the nurses asked. Her red hair was pinned up in a no-nonsense bun and she had the kind of pinched features that made her look perpetually constipated.

"Of course it's a circle. What else would it be?"

Another nurse tilted her head to examine the shape. "I'd say it's more oblong."

"Reminds me of an egg," a third nurse said. He rubbed his stomach. "I think I'm just hungry."

I shifted to my knees, rubbed out two parts of the chalk line, and redrew them.

"Much better," said the red-haired nurse.

My gaze swept the area. "Nobody breaches the circle, oval, egg, or whatever you want to call it. Got it?"

Heads bobbed in agreement and I shifted my focus to the spell. I'd never performed one like this before and I prayed to the gods that I could.

I withdrew the travel wand from my handbag. I hadn't thought much of it when Aster and Linnea had given it to me, but there was something to be said for retractable wands.

I cleared my mind of all distractions—Aunt Hyacinth, the ring, the patients—and focused my will. Ivy's magic stirred before rising to greet me. At some point I would need to stop thinking of it as Ivy's and acknowledge that it now belonged to me, but today was not that day.

"*Imperium*," I chanted.

I felt the power grow. It started in my core as a small, compact ball that opened like a blossoming flower. It spread to my limbs, causing my fingers and toes to tingle with energy.

I held the wand in both hands in an upright position. Magic poured into the wand until the end glowed with a powerful white light.

"*Imperium*," I repeated, this time with more force.

Magic exploded from the tip of the wand and scattered into the air like silent fireworks. There was a moment of dense silence, as though the whole world had come to a complete stop. Then the lights flickered once before returning to full bloom. The sound of beeping filled the air as the life-saving machines began to function.

The staff members cheered. One of the nurses threw his arms around my neck. "I don't know how to thank you."

"How about directing me to the floor with the food poisoning victims?"

He pointed up. "Third floor. We admitted about a dozen yesterday. As far as I know, we haven't released anyone yet."

I took the next stairwell to the next floor. The lights on this floor were flickering, which suggested the coven was still working in the lobby to restore power. I'd join them as soon as I finished my investigation.

I paused at the central station and addressed a druid healer in a blue smock. "I'm looking for a patient named Artie. Food poisoning."

She crooked a finger. "This way."

I followed her to a room further along the corridor. "We have a dozen patients from the same restaurant. They were all severely dehydrated and in need of fluids," the healer explained.

"Thanks." I knocked on the doorjamb before entering. "Excuse me. Are you Artie?"

The shifter looked at me and grunted. He wore a paper-thin hospital gown and was curled into the fetal position. I was glad he was facing me or I was pretty sure I'd have a full view of his backside.

"He's on the mend," the healer said, smiling. "He's just grumpy about the whole experience."

"What kind of hospital loses power?" Artie grumbled. "Starry Hollow isn't some backwater town."

I cut a glance at the healer. "Any update on the source of the illness?"

She shook her head. "The whole thing is odd. The

patients were all admitted around the same time with the same symptoms, but they didn't eat the same meals."

"I had shrimp," Artie said. He repositioned himself so he was flat on his back. "My roommate had gnocchi."

"We made a comprehensive list of each patient's order and, while there's some overlap, there's no commonality," the healer continued.

That settled it for me. The illness had been caused by the Ring of Despair.

"Did you happen to notice anyone at the restaurant wearing an aquamarine ring?" I asked Artie.

His brow furrowed. "What? You think someone carried poison in a ring like they did in old spy movies?"

"That would explain why only certain paranormals became ill despite eating different dishes," the healer said.

I didn't want to set off a wave of panic. "It's a possibility."

"Tell me when you find out who's responsible so I can express my gratitude," Artie said, practically snarling.

"I take it you didn't notice the ring," I said.

"No, but I'm not one to notice jewelry. You might want to ask Mr. Gnocchi over here."

I ventured further into the room to see another shifter curled into a ball. "No ring," he said softly. "Only saw a pretty necklace on the lady at the next table. Probably three karats." He shivered.

I walked closer and pulled up the blanket. "You like jewelry?"

"I like the flashy pieces. My mom was a performer."

I left a business card on the bedside table. "If you remember an aquamarine ring, will you contact me?"

He nodded, but his focus was clearly on feeling like garbage.

I patted the blanket. "Feel better."

I left the hospital with determined steps. It was time to think outside the proverbial box.

I had to find this ring before it was too late.

# CHAPTER SIXTEEN

When I finally arrived home, Marley jumped on me, eager to hear how events unfolded at the hospital.

"We make a great team," she said.

Raoul scowled. *There's no M in R&R.*

*That's R for Rose, remember? You're the one who suggested she might want to join the business someday.*

*I didn't mean today*, he huffed. *I meant an indeterminate time in the future.*

"We learned about pendulums in divinations class at school and I think it could be helpful to you." Marley chattered on, oblivious to the raccoon's flare of jealousy.

I craned my neck to look at her. "Pendulums? Like a hypnotist who swings a pocket watch back and forth?"

"Same idea," Marley said. "It's great for binary questions." I must've looked blank because she added, "That means where the answer can only be a choice between two things, like yes or no questions."

"Oh, like the Guess What? game. How do we make a pendulum?"

"I'm so glad you asked." Marley popped up from the chair and disappeared into the kitchen. She returned a couple minutes later holding a tray laden with objects.

I sniffed the air. "Do I smell cinnamon?"

She set the tray on the dining table. "It'll be easier if we work over here."

Raoul and I joined her at the table. I noticed a cinnamon stick among the items, which explained the familiar scent.

Marley unzipped her backpack and retrieved a silver chain. "The teacher gave us each a chain of our own in class." She tied the cinnamon stick to the end of the chain and tested the weight. "Now we need to calibrate it."

"Calibrate a cinnamon stick?"

"It's not a cinnamon stick anymore. It's a pendulum." She held the chain aloft. "We need to ask a question where we know the answer will be yes. Then we'll know which direction is yes. We repeat the test with a question where we know the answer is no."

Raoul rubbed his paws together. *I've got one.* He leaned forward and addressed the pendulum. *Is Ember incompetent?* He turned to look at me. *Right? That's easy.*

I shook my head. "Does Raoul like pizza?"

The pendulum swung to the right. Marley returned the chain to a neutral position. "Now ask a definitive no question."

"Does pineapple belong on pizza?" I asked.

The pendulum swung in a tight circle.

"That's a general opinion that can go either way."

"Not in a world with any taste," I muttered.

"You need to rephrase it." Marley steadied the pendulum. "Does Ember believe that pineapple belongs on pizza?" The pendulum swung to the left. "There. Now we've calibrated it."

"Do you think I can use this instead of interviewing suspects?"

"That's the idea." Marley set the pendulum on the table. "What do you think?"

I nodded. "It won't hold up in court, but I could use it to gather information."

Marley beamed with pride. "I knew you'd like it. I couldn't wait to come home and tell you about it." She paused, her brow wrinkling in consternation. "Of course some of the other kids were using pendulums after school for the most immature reasons."

"Like what?"

"Bella used hers to ask Kiefer whether he liked Jasmine as more than a friend." Marley rolled her eyes. "Hunter asked his sister if he was getting a new pair of skis for his birthday."

"You're right. Using it to catch a thief is much better." Now that I had no suspects left to interview, the pendulum might be able to point me in the right direction.

Raoul gestured to my face. *Now that we've mastered that magic, can we do something about your affliction?*

I balked. "You mean the affliction *you* caused?"

Marley jumped to her feet. "Yes! I can help with that."

I frowned at her. "Seriously? Are they teaching magical cosmetology now?"

She licked her lips. "Actually I learned this one from eavesdropping on witches in the cafeteria. They're obsessed with perfecting their social media profile pictures."

"Why don't they use filters like every woman over thirty?"

"Because filters are obvious, according to Bella. If you use magic correctly, no one can identify the flaws."

Well, I certainly had more than my share of flaws at the moment. "Okay, what do you suggest I do to get rid of these marks?" It would be nice to stop looking like a recent escapee from a medieval plague.

Marley brightened. "Leave it to me." She hurried to the kitchen and returned with a selection of herbs, as well as a mortar and pestle. "Bella had an acne breakout and she swears by this."

I watched her deft fingers blend and mix a combination of herbs. She impressed me more each day with her knowledge and abilities.

Raoul leaned forward to examine the mixture. *Smells like the dump. Don't go walking in the woods smelling like this or you'll be mistaken for dinner.*

"Duly noted."

Marley applied the mixture to my skin. "Start with this and then if it works, I'll make more for the rest of your body."

I inhaled the gnarly aroma. "How long do I leave it on before I can wash it off?"

"Twenty minutes."

Okay, I could manage twenty minutes. I'd breathe through my mouth like Norman Wolfsberger, a kid in my third-grade class. He was the noisiest kid in the class, mainly because you heard every single breath he took.

*This is my cue to leave.*

"I thought you liked the smell of the dump."

*I do. That's why it's my cue to leave. I'm going to find a snack.*

After twenty minutes, I washed off the mixture and examined my face. The blemishes had vanished.

"Well done, Marley," I said.

She inspected my face. "Awesome. I love it when a plan comes together." Marley slung her backpack over her shoulder. "I'm going to my room. I have a lot of homework."

"Thanks for your help, sweetheart. I appreciate it."

I waited until I was alone to hold up the pendulum. "Did someone steal the Ring of Despair?"

The pendulum swung to the right. I figured it was worth

checking in the unlikely event the ring had fallen down a crack behind the sink or disappeared some other way.

I waited for the pendulum to return to a neutral position before asking my next question.

"Have I already spoken to the thief?"

The pendulum swung right again. Hmm. Should I simply run down the list of suspects until the pendulum swung right to reveal the thief? It seemed too easy. If it worked, then why weren't all crimes solved using basic pendulum magic? Every law enforcement office in every paranormal town in the world would have a witch with a pendulum on their staff. There had to be a catch or limitation. Magic was powerful, but if I'd learned anything since moving to Starry Hollow, it was that magic couldn't solve all our problems. Some things were designed to be endured or solved the old-fashioned way rather than by a magical solution.

I thought about the way I sometimes solved crimes when I worked at the newspaper. I spoke to paranormals for an article, usually about a murder victim. What if there was an article about the missing ring? Something that lured the thief out of the shadows? I tugged my phone from my pocket and sent a text. It couldn't hurt to put another plan into place.

The response was immediate. *Tonight at 11. Whitethorn. Come alone.*

Who else would I come with? Marley? He was ridiculous.

As I was about to wrap up, another question occurred to me. I pondered the cinnamon stick at the end of the chain, thinking of Bella's use of the pendulum. Okay, so maybe I wasn't a teenager, but that didn't mean I'd outgrown the need for validation.

"Was breaking up with Alec the right decision?" I whispered. My heart fluttered as the pendulum began to move. It swung to the right with such force that I nearly lost my grip on it.

I tucked the pendulum into the small compartment in my purse. Although I knew the answer already, a little magical confirmation was just what I needed.

Thanks to the strong breeze along the coastline, it was a bumpy landing as I arrived outside the Whitethorn. I needed to log more hours on my broomstick. I enjoyed flying, but the downside was the noisy wind drowned out any music I wanted to hear. As far as I was concerned, part of the joy of traveling somewhere was listening to music en route.

Bentley signaled to me from the shadows of a corner booth.

"Hey, stranger," I said, sliding into the booth. I made a noise of approval when I noticed the glass of red wine that awaited me.

Bentley wrapped his hands around a pint of ale and ducked his head. "I feel like we're spies having a clandestine meeting."

"Well, there's no way I was coming to the office." I tapped my thumb against the base of my glass. "How *is* everything at the office?"

"Exactly how you'd expect. Alec is moody. Tanya is catering to everyone's needs and Heloise…" He stopped abruptly.

"Who's Heloise?"

Bentley's cheeks grew flushed. "I wasn't going to mention her. Stupid ale."

"Well, you've opened the can of worms now." I sipped my wine and braced myself for the intel.

"We hired a junior reporter. Her name is Heloise Nero and she's a nymph."

"Which kind?"

"Water. Does it matter?"

"No, just curious." I took another sip. "Is she pretty?"

Bentley's sigh was imbued with exasperation. "I don't know."

"That's a yes."

He leaned back against the booth. "I know you didn't arrange this meeting to talk about the paper."

He was right. I'd ended the relationship with Alec and I had to put on my big girl panties and brush off any pangs of jealousy I might feel. It wasn't healthy. Besides, I truly wanted him to be happy. Whether he was capable of that or not, however, remained to be seen.

"No, of course not. It's a habit I need to break and I'm working on it," I acknowledged. A part of me would always love him. I just couldn't sustain a relationship with him.

The elf offered a sympathetic smile. "It's natural to be interested. When you have a relationship like yours, you're always going to care about each other to some degree."

"That's very mature, Bentley. Am I to credit Meadow for this change in mindset?"

His eyes turned to slits. "Haha. Very funny."

I exhaled and shook off the emotions I was feeling. There was a more important matter to address. "I need a favor."

"Okay," he said slowly.

"I need you to write an article for tomorrow's paper. Front page if you can swing it."

His eyebrows inched up. "You can't be serious. That's a pretty big favor."

"I know, but the fate of Starry Hollow depends on it." I told him about the stolen ring and its negative impact.

Bentley whistled. "I see what you mean."

Bittersteel flew over and perched on the back of the booth. "One True Witch," the parrot squawked.

"Good evening to you too," I greeted him.

"I thought I smelled a familiar scent." Captain Yellowjacket ambled over to the booth. The vampire pirate owned and operated the ancient pub. "Not in the mood to come over and say hello?"

"I wasn't hiding from you," I protested. "Bentley had already ordered for me."

"In need of a top up, lass?" he offered.

"Sure. Why not? Thanks, Duncan." I could spell my broom to take me home if need be, although I doubted it would be necessary.

He ambled back to the bar and the parrot landed on his shoulder.

I turned my focus back to Bentley. "I'm trying to flush out the thief and that involves you writing a story about the theft of the ring and giving the ring a fake history."

Bentley leaned forward. "I'm listening."

"I need you to craft a story about the ring that includes a cleansing ritual."

The elf beamed. "I've always wanted to write fiction like Alec."

"Write whatever you want with the details, as long as you say the magic of the ring only works if you cleanse it in the shallow waters of the sea at these coordinates during a full moon." I slid over a piece of paper with the numbers.

Bentley grinned. "And the next full moon is in two nights."

"Exactly."

"Where are the coordinates for?"

"The cove up the road. It's secluded enough and there's a good place for me to hide. Plus it's at the water's edge so the thief won't be able to escape easily."

"Clever, Ember."

"If I'm right and the thief took the ring for its magic, they must be feeling desperate for it to work at this point. I'm going to wait and hope they show up with the ring."

"What if they don't see the article?"

I shrugged. "Nothing ventured, nothing gained. I'll keep investigating."

He nodded. "It's a good plan."

"I'd leave copies of the paper at all the places that have been touched by the ring so far." I named the restaurant, as well as the hospital, although hopefully all the food poisoning patients would be released by tomorrow.

Bentley emptied his pint glass and smacked his lips together. "I'm glad you've landed on your feet, Ember. It sucks what happened."

"I don't know that I've landed on my feet." More like sideways on my hip bone. "I'm okay though. What doesn't kill us makes us annoyed."

He squinted at me. "Don't you mean stronger?"

"That too."

"I hate to admit it, but I miss having you in the office."

I felt a rush of tenderness for the elf. Bentley was the brother I never wanted—until I didn't have him anymore. "You're welcome to irritate me in my new office anytime."

He perked up. "New office? Where's that?"

I gave him the address.

"Isn't that an empty plot of land?"

"It is until I put my she-shed there."

Bentley laughed. "Only you."

"How's married life?"

He fondled his pint glass. "It suits me."

"Yeah, I can see that. I bet she dotes on you."

"And I dote on her. We're equal opportunity doters."

"That's nice to hear."

A loud voice drifted over from the bar area. "You have to come to the wedding. She's my sister. I need a date. You know Fatima will be there."

I looked over to see a shifter with light brown hair talking to a petite blonde.

"And what?" the petite blonde asked. "I'm your buffer."

Holy Hera. Talk about a gift horse. I held up a finger to Bentley. "Gimme one sec. I'll be right back." I sauntered over to the bar. "You're Lindsey's brother, Greg."

His gaze skimmed over me. "Yeah. Who are you?"

His girlfriend inched closer to him and hugged his chest as though I was about to make out with him if she didn't create a physical barrier. Don't worry, girlfriend. I have no interest in deadbeat dads.

"Rose MacGuffin," I lied. "I work as a consultant for the MRS." MRS stood for Magical Revenue Service, the paranormal version of the IRS.

He flinched. "And?"

"And this is your official notice that you're under investigation for fraud."

His gaze swept the room. "You're giving me notice in a pub?"

"Provision 13(b)(1) states that official notice must be given face-to-face, but that's the extent of the requirement." A complete fabrication that I had no doubt Greg was too lazy to double-check.

"What kind of fraud? I pay my taxes."

"But you don't pay your child support. You've been in arrears for a year now. Once you hit that twelve-month mark, it automatically triggers an MRS investigation because where there's financial fraud in one area, we have found there's likely fraud in another."

He paled considerably. I had to admit, the look on his face was gratifying.

"What…How do I rectify that?" he stammered.

His girlfriend punched his chest. "You haven't paid child support in a year?"

"I can explain," he said. "I had to buy you that car…"

Her eyes narrowed. "You didn't have to buy me anything. You acted like it was chump change to you."

"I just wanted to make you happy, baby."

"I'm not your baby." She shoved him away. "You have babies that you don't take care of. What kind of loser are you?"

He wore a pleading expression. "I would never do that to you. You're my angel."

"Yeah, right. Until I get knocked up and you get bored and move on to the next fool. No thanks." She marched out of the pub.

"There's an easy way to fix this," I told him.

He continued to stare at the empty doorway, as though willing her to come back.

"Greg?"

He turned to me and sighed in resignation. "Yeah. I'll take care of it first thing in the morning."

I clapped him on the shoulder. "Once we receive confirmation of payment, we'll process compliance on our end." I paused. "You should know that because you triggered the audit, you don't get another twelve months next time. Payment must be made on time each month or the audit goes straight back into effect." And I had a feeling Greg had plenty to hide. He seemed like the kind of guy who cheated in every area of his life where he thought he could get away with it.

"Noted." His shoulders slumped, he turned and left the pub.

"That was quite the spectacle," Captain Yellowjacket said.

"It was long past due."

"Aye. I imagine so from what I heard. Did the ex-wife hire you?"

I smiled at him. "No. I consider this a public service."

The vampire pirate nodded his approval and handed me a

full glass of wine. "You're a good lass, Ember Rose, no matter what your aunt tells everyone."

Right. My aunt. "I do my best." I didn't always succeed, but at least I could look at my reflection in the mirror every day and not feel a deep sense of shame. That had to count for something.

# CHAPTER SEVENTEEN

I STOOD in a clearing in the woods and focused on my breathing. It felt strange to be out here practicing on my own, instead of under the watchful eye of one of my coven tutors. Now that I had Ivy's power in addition to my own, I felt obligated to learn to wield it responsibly. Sort of like Spider-Man, with great power from an ancestor who hid her magic to avoid it being taken comes great responsibility.

Magic flowed through my veins as easily as blood. It wasn't enough to have access to it. I needed to better understand it.

Before I could fully immerse myself, Simon came into view. I considered the butler a trusted friend, despite his loyalty to Aunt Hyacinth.

"Hey. What are you doing out here?" I asked.

He inhaled deeply. "Fresh air is good for the soul."

I folded my arms. "She sent you to spy on me, didn't she? What does she think I'm going to do out here?"

Simon shrugged. "She's a curious witch, you know that. Likes to keep a finger on the pulse of Starry Hollow."

"More like her heel on its neck."

He ambled over to one of the large live oak trees and rested his back. "So what *are* you doing?"

"Are you asking for her or for you?" I waved him off. "It doesn't matter. I'm practicing magic. It's not quite the same without Marigold marching in front of me and snapping orders, but it's better than nothing."

Simon gave me an appraising look. "And here she's been so concerned you'll squander the gift."

"Honestly, I'd rather squander it than use it to bend everyone to my will."

Simon wore a vague smile. "How do you intend to use it?"

"I don't. I want to know that if the situation requires it, I can rise to the challenge without making a complete mess." Or even worse, hurting someone.

"She only wants the best for you."

"No. She only wants the best for her. The rest of us deserve scraps. She's basically the Marie Antoinette of magic."

Simon peeled himself off the tree. "Would you like a practice partner?"

"Won't she whip you for insubordination?"

He removed his tweed jacket and hung it on a branch. "What my mistress doesn't know won't hurt her." He unbuttoned his sleeves and pushed them to his elbows. "I'm at your service, Miss Ember. What would you like to work on?"

"How about a transmogrification spell?" If I had a willing subject, why not?

"Very well then. Not a spider, please."

I cracked a smile. "I didn't realize spiders were an issue for you."

"And now I've revealed a weakness." He clucked his tongue. "I should know better."

"Don't worry, Simon. Unlike Hyacinth, I'd never use it against you." My aunt exploited weaknesses with the same

# MAGIC & MISFORTUNE

enthusiasm and energy that Wyatt Nash reserved for beautiful women. That wasn't my style, no matter how powerful I was.

"I know it seems that way to you, but my mistress doesn't wield her power mindlessly. She always has a reason for what she does."

"And sometimes that reason is 'because she feels like it.'"

"I won't argue with you, miss. Under the circumstances, I can understand your point of view." He planted his feet hip-width apart. "Je suis prest."

I faltered. "That's the Rose motto."

"Not quite. Your family's motto is *carpe noctem*."

Oops. Right. Seize the night. When Marley and I first arrived in town, I'd been delighted to dine at Thornhold and learn our family motto and see our crest. Marley and I had been alone in the world until my cousins came for us. Suddenly we found ourselves thrust into another family's life —*our* family—and I had welcomed the change with open arms.

"Did I say something wrong, miss?" Simon asked, observing my expression.

I brushed it off. "No. I just remembered something, that's all." I brandished my wand. "Let's begin."

The magic moved quickly, as though it had been waiting patiently for me to summon it forth. I simply aimed my wand and magic ripped through me before I could utter the necessary word.

I watched in disbelief as Simon morphed into a furry brown creature.

A squirrel.

I'd chosen a squirrel, so that part was correct, but usually I had to say the word out loud in Latin—*sciurus*. This time the magic burst from me before I had a chance. It seemed the focused thought was enough to cause the transformation.

"Look how cute you are," I cooed.

The squirrel surprised me by bolting from the clearing.

"Oh, nuts!"

I ran after him, but he scampered up one of the large oak trees. "Simon, come back!"

I stood on my tiptoes and tried to catch a glimpse of him. I expected him to retain his own thoughts, but I must've used too much power because Simon seemed to think he was an actual squirrel. Even worse, he looked like every other squirrel in the woods.

Great Goddess of the Moon. I had to change him back or Aunt Hyacinth would think I did it on purpose.

"Simon!"

Three squirrels chased each other across the branches. Ugh. Which one was Simon? Couldn't one of them at least have a bald spot to help me identify him?

The squirrels jumped from one tree to the next. With my head tipped back, I began to feel dizzy as I tried to keep track of them.

*Is there a problem?*

Raoul appeared in the clearing, dragging a rusty shovel behind him. Bonkers circled above his head.

I nodded toward the shovel. "Dare I ask?"

He dropped it on the ground. *Seems like you have more important matters.*

I heaved a sigh. "Simon is a squirrel and I have no idea which one."

Raoul snickered. *Dare I ask?*

"I need turn him back before Hyacinth finds out. She sent him to spy on me, but he offered to help me practice instead."

*And this is how you repay his kindness?* The raccoon clucked his tongue.

I glared at him. "Obviously I didn't mean to completely

turn him. I sank too much magic into the spell. That's the whole point of practicing."

Bonkers landed on a low branch and meowed.

*We can both help*, Raoul said. *Bonkers can chase the squirrels toward us and you and I can catch them.*

"In what?"

*I don't know. You're the powerful witch. Make a magical force-field or something.*

I raced through the magical possibilities and settled on a spell. "Okay, I'm ready." I twirled my finger in the air. "Bonkers, do your thing."

The winged cat swooped from the branch and soared to the other side of the trio of squirrels.

Energy pulsed through me and I prepared to lob a handful of magic.

Bonkers hissed loudly at the squirrels and they leaped into action, springing toward me.

"That's right, little buddies. Come to mama," I urged.

Raoul stayed beside me, ready to act as a defense. If one of the squirrels managed to bypass the spell, the raccoon was prepared to catch it.

Before they could break away, I hit all three squirrels at once with a reversal spell. They flashed with white light and the middle one with the acorn in his mouth exploded into Simon.

He spat out the acorn. "What happened?"

"You don't remember?"

He examined his hands. "Was I a squirrel?"

"I'm afraid so. If it's any consolation, you made two new friends." I gestured to the two squirrels still in the clearing. Aware of our attention, the squirrels darted away.

Simon brushed off his sleeves. "I'm glad you're practicing."

"I'm sorry. I didn't intend to do a complete transformation."

He retrieved his tweed jacket and folded it over his arm. "I would be more than happy to assist you in future practice sessions."

"Don't feel obligated. I don't want you to get in trouble with the big H." If his treachery was discovered, my aunt was liable to turn him into something much worse than a squirrel as punishment.

He bowed slightly. "It will be under the guise of performing my surveillance duties. My mistress will be none the wiser." He turned on his heel and vacated the clearing. I noticed his butt twitch as he walked away and wondered whether it was the after effects of losing his bushy tail.

"Now do you want to tell me why you need a shovel?" I asked.

Raoul didn't get a chance to answer. Thundering footsteps shook the ground and drew my attention behind me. They sounded like they were coming from the direction of the pond. I shot a quizzical look at Raoul.

*It's those wild horses finally coming to try and drag me away.*

"From what?"

He held up his paws. *Tacos, pizza, my CD of Air Supply's Greatest Hits. You name it.*

I frowned. "You have a CD of Air Supply's Greatest Hits? How am I only discovering this now?" And how could someone throw away such a treasure?

The thundering intensified and a group of animals burst through the trees. Rabbits, foxes, deer, beavers, and mice rushed past us like that scene in Jurassic Park when the other dinosaurs were running for their lives from a T-Rex.

A turtle crawled behind them.

I nudged Raoul. "Ask him what's going on."

The raccoon dropped to his stomach and crawled alongside the turtle. By the time he finished, I didn't need his answer because I already had one.

Raoul dragged himself to his hind legs and followed my gaze to the darkening sky. The wind began to howl, bending trees to its will.

"Great Mother of Abraham Lincoln," I said. Thanks to a magical weather bubble, Starry Hollow was blessed with perfect weather most of the time. There were no unexpected storms, certainly not the kind that resulted in a stampede of woodland creatures.

Thunder boomed and this time it had nothing to do with scampering animals. Lightning flashed in the sky, followed quickly by another white-hot bolt that struck a nearby tree.

I grabbed Raoul's paw. "We need to get inside. Now."

I lifted the raccoon into my arms and ran. The heavens opened and rain fell from black clouds, pelting us. I felt like we were under attack. By the time we made it to the cottage, we were both soaked to the bone.

*Holy hellfire*, the raccoon said. He dropped on the floor in front of the door, too drained to take another step.

It took me a minute to catch my breath. Thunder rolled over the cottage. The lights flickered and I worried we'd lose power too. At least I knew how to fix it.

"Marley," I called. My daughter had been terrified of thunderstorms in the human world.

I took the steps two at a time until I reached her bedroom doorway. I spotted a large lump under the blankets. PP3 sat on top of the lump like a misplaced stone gargoyle.

I sat on the edge of the bed and rubbed the blanket. "Hey, it's okay."

Slowly the blanket peeled down, revealing Marley's head. "What's going on? We never get bad storms here."

"I think it's the Ring of Despair."

She pushed down the blanket and pulled herself to a seated position. "How long will this last?"

"Hopefully it's just a passing storm."

"You're a weather witch. Can't you make it stop?"

I wasn't exactly a weather witch, but I knew what she meant. In times of great stress, I'd demonstrated the ability to control the elements. It was how I escaped from Jimmy the Lighter the first time he tried to hurt me. I'd conjured a storm without realizing it.

"I don't think I can fight this," I said. "Let's give it time and see if it passes."

Within half an hour, the clouds parted and beams of sunlight returned. Marley and I watched from the kitchen window, sipping from mugs of hot chocolate. I'd changed clothes and threatened to use the hair dryer on Raoul, which prompted him to shut himself in the oven until I promised to leave him be. I left a towel on the floor outside the oven.

*No hot chocolate for me?* The raccoon appeared beside us, wrapped in the blue towel.

"Cowards don't get hot chocolate."

*I wasn't afraid.*

I gave him a pointed look. "You huddled in the corner of the bathroom and begged for mercy."

He crossed his short arms. *Okay, fine. I was terrified of my fur getting sucked into the little motor at the back of the hair dryer. Can you blame me? It's like sticking your head in front of whirring helicopter blades and hoping for the best.*

"And your alternative was to stick yourself in an oven?"

*It wasn't on.*

Shaking my head, I crossed the kitchen to the island and prepared a third mug of hot chocolate.

"Mom, you have to find the ring. What if next time it's a tsunami or a hurricane?"

A similar thought had crossed my mind, but I hadn't wanted to say it out loud. Marley was anxious enough.

"I'm doing my best," I said.

I added a handful of tiny marshmallows to the drink and set it on the table for Raoul. He wasted no time devouring it.

"Maybe we should ask Aunt Hyacinth for help," Marley said.

I choked on saliva. "Are you feeling okay?"

Marley rinsed her empty mug and placed it in the dishwasher. "I'm serious, Mom. You have Ivy's power, but she has experience. Maybe together you can find the ring and stop the spread of the despair or whatever it is."

"Honey, even if I was willing, I don't think Aunt Hyacinth would be. She's the one who decided to draw a line in the sand, remember?"

"But wouldn't she put aside her feelings for the greater good?"

My heart squeezed at the look of pure innocence on my daughter's face. She still saw the best in everyone, whereas I saw a cranky old witch who only acted in her own best interest.

"I can do this without help, Marley."

She lodged no further objections. "Don't forget you have that party tonight."

I knew what she was thinking. That maybe I'd run into Aunt Hyacinth and casually drop the hint that I was fighting a force greater than myself.

"I remember, thanks. Are you sure you'll be fine on your own?" Marley had been doing really well staying home alone, but I had no doubt the unexpected thunderstorm had thrown her for a loop.

She offered a reassuring smile. "I'll be fine. My homework is finished. I have a dog to snuggle and a book to read. What more does a girl need?"

Inwardly I sighed with relief. Mrs. Babcock was no longer an option anyway. The brownie served my aunt, which meant she no longer offered childcare services.

"Which book are you reading? Something for school?"

Her smile faded. "No."

Her evasive tone didn't escape me. "Marley?"

She bit her lip, debating whether to be truthful. I knew my daughter, though. Marley was honest to a fault.

"It's one of Alec's books."

That explained the guilty look. "It's okay to read his books, sweetheart."

"Are you sure? I don't want to upset you by having reminders around the house. I've been hiding it under my pillow."

My chest ached. My daughter was compassion personified. "I'm a grown woman in charge of my own emotions. It's not your job to protect me."

Marley seemed to mull over my response, as though weighing its veracity. "Okay," she finally said. "You should probably wash your hair before the party." She touched two spots on her own head. "You have a few twigs in it."

Raoul moved closer to examine me. *Ooh, I think I see bird poop too.*

"What?" My hands flew to my hair.

*You can hardly blame them. They were flying for their lives. You'd sh...*

I cut him off with a hard look. "I'd do nothing of the kind. I'm going upstairs to shower. If you'd like to stay and keep Marley company tonight, feel free."

After showering and carefully removing evidence of the woods from my hair, I put on a simple wrap dress in dark blue. As the party was outdoors, I opted for a pair of sensible sandals, although the ground would likely be muddy after the earlier deluge.

MAGIC & MISFORTUNE

I admired my reflection in the mirror. That'll do, pig. That'll do.

I used a basic spell to smooth the frizz from my hair and applied minimal makeup—a coat of lipstick and mascara. At some point I'd have to start paying attention to wrinkle cream and all the other lotions and potions that came with aging not-so-gracefully, but today was not that day.

Marley gave me a long look. "You look pretty, but why are you even going to a birthday party for Reed? Isn't he the one you think is creepy?"

Reed Rider-Lilly was an older wizard in the coven known for frequent bouts of correctile dysfunction. If someone asked a question, Reed was sure to restate your answer as though you were incapable of speaking intelligibly.

"It's one of the things we do as adults. Attend social functions against our will."

"You made me go to Nolan Rogers' birthday party in fourth grade and I didn't want to go."

"Because I was worried no one else would be there." Nolan was one of those kids who would've looked completely at home in lederhosen and a feather cap.

"It was a roller-skating rink, remember? You made me wear a dress and I fell over and everyone saw my underpants."

"Hey, at least they were cute. They were white with little purple flowers."

Marley's brow creased. "I'm disturbed that you remember the underpants in such detail."

"Need I remind you that I bought every pair you owned? Of course I remember."

"Everyone called me Purple Panties for months afterward." Marley shuddered. "Nightmare."

"Well, I'm wearing a dress to this party and if I fall over,

171

it'll be much worse because I'll be treating everyone to my bare butt."

Marley cringed. "Why are you not wearing any underpants?"

"Because they make me look lumpy in this dress."

"Do you think you'll speak to Aunt Hyacinth if you see her?"

I smoothed the sides of the dress. "I'm going to play it by ear."

"Too bad you're not going with Alec. He always sends a limo."

I had the same thought earlier, but I pushed it aside. Limos and fancy dinners had been perks of the relationship, but they hadn't been as important to me as Alec himself.

"Life goes on," I said.

Marley rolled her eyes. "If you start singing ob-la-di-ob-la-da, I'll be forced to use my wand on you."

I smiled at her. "Are you threatening your mother with magical violence?"

She gave a nonchalant shrug. "You know what they say—spare the wand, spoil the mother."

"Uh huh." I plucked my purse from the table and slung it over my shoulder. "Text me if you need anything."

Raoul raised a paw. *If you haven't already ordered the pizza for delivery, now might be a good time.*

I shut the door behind me without a backward glance.

# CHAPTER EIGHTEEN

The moment I approached the party tent set up in the clearing, I began to have misgivings about my attendance. There was the issue of the ring, of course. There was also the issue that everyone from the coven seemed to be here. It was one thing to be surrounded by everyone at the monthly meetings, but I could jet in and out without making small talk. A party atmosphere, on the other hand, required conversation. It didn't help that my sandals kept sinking into the soft earth.

Gardenia was the first witch to spot me. She was the coven scribe, which meant she was very organized and had an eye for detail. Basically, she was the opposite of me.

"Ember, how delightful to see you. I thought for sure you'd sit this one out."

I blinked. "Oh? Why is that?"

"I heard you were suffering from a terrible affliction." Her brow furrowed as she scrutinized me, presumably checking for evidence of horns or scales.

I forced a smile. "As you can see, I'm perfectly healthy."

"How about that thunderstorm earlier? Wasn't that remarkable?"

"It really was."

Her voice dropped to a whisper. "I hear the Council of Elders are calling an emergency meeting tomorrow night to determine the cause."

Ugh. I didn't want the Council of Elders involved, especially not when Aunt Hyacinth was a member. I had to find that ring before the council commandeered my case.

I held up the gift bag. "Where are we dropping the presents for the wizard of honor?"

She turned and pointed. "That table over there. You can't miss it. The huge present in the middle is from your aunt." It rose from the surface of the table like a middle finger.

"Thank you." I ventured over and set my small gift bag gingerly on the table, right next to the box from Aunt Hyacinth.

"He's going to love my gift." My aunt's voice floated over to me and I stiffened. "It was more than I'd been planning to spend, but when you have as much money as I do, why not spend it on those who matter?"

I rolled my eyes. "Yes, because the name Reed is so important to you. I once heard you refer to him as a potato with magic."

Aunt Hyacinth suppressed a smile. "That *was* clever, wasn't it?" She resembled Mother Earth in a green kaftan with swirls of brown and red. Bright red boots poked out from beneath the hem of the kaftan. Unsurprisingly, my aunt had come prepared for the muddy ground.

"Why are you speaking to me?"

"I thought it would be nice to catch up. Tell me, dear, how is your new venture faring? Must be so difficult to operate without an office."

I refused to give her the satisfaction of making a scene. "I'm managing."

"The way you managed in New Jersey?"

There was so much venom infused in that simple question. I was relieved when Iris interrupted us. There was no telling what my response might've been.

"Ember, I'm so happy to see you." Iris sailed across the clearing and enveloped me in a hug. "I've been telling everyone about your assistance at the hospital." She released me, keeping one arm wrapped around my shoulders. "Hyacinth, your niece was a superstar. She had the critical floor up and running before the rest of us had a chance to draw breath."

Aunt Hyacinth's lips formed a tight smile. "Well, she is a Rose. I'd expect nothing less."

"I can't imagine what caused both systems to fail," Iris said, seemingly oblivious to the tension. "That's never happened in the history of the hospital."

"Much like this recent thunderstorm," my aunt said.

Iris sucked in a breath. "Yes, wasn't it incredible? I would've enjoyed it had I not been in the middle of a yoga session at the cliff. I don't think I've ever run so fast in my life."

"The council is meeting tomorrow night to get to the bottom of it," Aunt Hyacinth said.

"Be sure to sing your niece's praises to them when you're there." Iris gave me a squeeze. "What a wonderful witch you've become, Ember. And to think you grew up without magic. Imagine the kind of witch you'd be now if you'd been raised here." She let go and waved to someone in the crowd. "I'll catch up with your later, Hyacinth. I'd like to discuss a budgetary matter." Iris maneuvered through the guests, leaving Hyacinth and I alone again.

"Yes, imagine the witch you could've been if your father hadn't been so foolish," my aunt murmured.

"Hardly foolish. My father was trying to prevent me from becoming *you*."

She scowled. "Your father had it easy. I was the one…" Her eyes closed briefly as she seemed to clamp down on her emotions. "This is a party. We should enjoy it." She sauntered away without a backward glance.

"What was that about?" Wren Stanton-Summer appeared beside me.

"The usual family drama."

He handed me a full glass of wine. "Sorry. I don't see anything stronger."

"Thanks. This will do." I surveyed the guests. "Where's Delphine?"

"She's mingling. Calla trapped her in a corner to ask about a nonfiction book she wants added to the library. I cut and run."

I elbowed him in the ribs. "You're not supposed to abandon your damsel in her hour of need. Get back in there and rescue her."

He chuckled. "Delphine's fine. You know she loves to talk about books. I had to save myself."

"You two seem to be going strong." I drank a mouthful of wine. It was a dry, full-bodied red. Just what the healer ordered.

He gazed at her across the room. "She's a marvel. I feel like the luckiest wizard in the world." He craned his neck. "Is that your cousin trailing after Honey Avens-Beech?"

I twisted to see Florian falling in step with Honey, who seemed bored by his mere presence. Poor Florian. The tables had finally been turned. I had to admit, I was curious to see how this would play out. I'd yet to meet a woman who was able to resist his charms.

"We had a double date with Honey and her brother. Florian seems to have developed a crush."

Wren's brow shot up. "You went out with Castor? Why is this the first I'm hearing about it?"

"It was only a couple days ago."

"I know, but this is Starry Hollow. I'm surprised I didn't hear about it before you paid the bill."

I laughed. "It was just dinner."

"Two eligible Roses and two eligible members of the Avens-Beech family?" He produced a low whistle. "That's a strategy session."

"As far as I'm concerned, it was a pleasant meal and nothing more."

Wren observed Honey from a distance. "Honey is an accomplished witch. Graduated top of her class."

"I think she's going to be Florian's white whale. He's definitely smitten, but she's not interested. I get the sense she'd rather date Bill Gates than George Clooney—and not because of the money."

"It'll be good for Florian to experience rejection for once in his privileged life. It builds character."

"I agree." I took another sip of wine. "And it's entertaining to watch too."

"What's entertaining to watch? Are you watching baby frogs try to hop across lily pads again?" Marigold joined us by the gift table. "She spent an hour during one of our lessons laughing at the frogs instead of mastering psychic skills."

"The frogs were more interesting." I had to admit, it was nice to see her again. Ever since my aunt withdrew my coven tutors, everyone had been afraid to be seen with me and incur Hyacinth's wrath.

Marigold leaned closer. "Have you been practicing on your own?"

"Not practicing per se, but I've been using magic as part of my job."

"Right. The detective agency or whatever it is." The witch seemed less than impressed.

I dipped into my purse and produced a business card. "We're open for business. Tell your friends."

Marigold scanned the card. "R&R?"

"Rose and Raoul."

She stifled a laugh. "Only you would go into business with a raccoon."

"He's not just a raccoon. He's my familiar and he has a helpful skill set."

"I don't think eating to excess counts as a skill set," Marigold said.

"Ah, look. The gang's all here." Hazel raised her arms as she approached us. The crazed clown looked less crazed and clownish than usual tonight, thanks to toned-down makeup and a sleeker hairstyle.

"Ian's over there," I said, pointing to the buffet table. "Should we call him over to complete the set?" I watched as the wizard stuffed an entire lobster roll in his mouth. "On second thought, maybe later."

"I suppose you haven't practiced your runes."

"I can't even pretend to miss the Big Book of Scribbles," I said.

Hazel smoothed back a stray red curl. "No, manners were never your strong suit."

"Blame Aunt Hyacinth for not assigning me a manners tutor. The moment she found out I was from New Jersey, she should've assembled a team."

Wren grunted. "As much as I complained about them, I miss our lessons."

I pivoted to face him. "You complained about lessons with *me*?"

The wizard smirked. "What? You thought you were the only one who'd been put upon?"

I grasped for a response. Yes, as a matter of fact I did think that. On the other hand, nobody liked being bullied by Aunt Hyacinth. They'd agreed to tutor me because they had no real choice in the matter.

Wren bent over to whisper in my ear, "Big smile. Here comes your future husband."

The crowd seemed to part like the Red Sea as Castor Avens-Beech made his way toward me. Admittedly the wizard looked handsome in a tailored dark blue suit with a crimson tie, but—much like Honey and Florian—I simply wasn't interested.

"Ember, you look splendid," Castor said. He greeted me with a kiss on the cheek. "That dress is stunning on you."

"Thank you. That's a nice suit."

Marigold and Hazel smiled at him like two hungry hyenas.

"You know Hazel and Marigold," I said, hoping to snap them to attention.

"And Wren too, of course," Castor said, shaking Wren's hand.

"I haven't seen you in Starry Hollow for ages," Marigold said.

Castor caught the eye of a passing waiter and beckoned him to us. "I've been traveling extensively, but you know what they say—there's no place like home."

The waiter lowered the tray of canapés and we each took a sample.

"Thank you," I said.

"Stay with us," Hazel instructed the waiter. "You've only got a few left. We'll help you out so you don't need to keep circulating."

"Your family must be pleased to have you back," Marigold said.

"They think thirty is that special age where you settle down and start a family of your own." Castor didn't sound particularly enthusiastic. No wonder he'd been to see Artemis. He was going through the motions to please his parents rather than because *he* felt ready.

"Any lucky ladies in the running?" Marigold asked.

Castor gave me the kind of smile that would've melted Marigold's panties if it had been directed at her. "I had the distinct pleasure of dining with this incredible woman recently. I'm hoping to do it again soon."

It seemed the love bomb wasn't the cause of his interest after all.

Hazel snatched the last canapé off the tray and shoved it into her mouth to stifle a moan.

Marigold grabbed the empty tray from the waiter's hands and fanned herself with it. "Hot flash," she explained apologetically.

"There must be so many coven members you want to catch up with. Don't let us keep you," I said. That was Starry Hollow-speak for 'this conversation is finished.'

"There are, but none as fascinating as you."

Oh, he was smooth.

Wren lowered his gaze to the floor so that Castor couldn't see his amused grin.

"I wouldn't linger too long or someone will be handing out 'save the date' cards before we leave here tonight," I warned.

"A dance later?" Castor asked.

"Only if it's the funky chicken," I said.

A passing witch grabbed his arm and trilled with delight. "Castor, finally! Your mother told me you'd be here. I've been searching everywhere for you. There's a lovely witch I'd like you to meet." Castor shot me a helpless look as she pulled him across the room.

"On that note, I'm going to find Delphine before the dancing starts." Wren slipped away and left me with Hazel and Marigold.

Marigold tugged my sleeve. "I didn't know Castor was interested in you."

"It's a recent development."

"I'm surprised," Hazel said. "The Avens-Beech family is as keen on pedigree as Hyacinth. If you're the black sheep, you're hardly marriage material."

"I'm not marriage material because I'm not interested in a romantic relationship with Castor," I pointed out.

Hazel spoke in a hushed tone. "Why? What's wrong with him? I've always suspected he had a deep, dark secret."

"Like a third nipple," Marigold added. "Not that I'd object to that."

Hazel shot her a curious look. "I was thinking more along the lines of a shady past."

"He's not old enough to have a shady past," Marigold said.

I observed Castor as he mixed and mingled. "He's perfectly respectable as far as I can tell."

"Then why no interest?" Marigold asked. "He's a handsome wizard from a good family. The match might bring you back into Hyacinth's good graces."

"You seem to be under the misguided impression that I *want* to worm my way back into her good graces. Aunt Hyacinth is toxic and I've been working on extricating myself from those relationships."

"She's still your aunt," Hazel said, as though that simple fact should be enough.

"And she'll be my aunt until the day she dies, but until she changes her behavior, there'll be no reconciliation."

Marigold and Hazel exchanged uneasy glances.

Florian approached us. Correction: he moped. "Honey won't dance with me."

"Be a good wizard and take no for an answer."

He appeared genuinely baffled. "I don't understand. Everyone wants to dance with me. There's usually a queue. Why doesn't she want to?"

"Maybe because there's a queue."

He rubbed the back of his neck. "It's like marketing. When you see seven other women are interested in the same guy, you're going to want to check him out."

"You're not a toaster oven, Florian. That's not how relationships work."

He sighed. "What can I do to woo her?"

"Nothing. Leave her alone." I thought of Lynda's wise words. *If you love someone, let them go. If they return, they were always yours. If they don't, they were never yours to begin with.* Although Florian's feelings weren't quite at the level of love, the same premise applied.

"But how will she learn how awesome I am if she doesn't get to know me?"

"Honey is a smart, independent witch. She's not going to think you're awesome if you keep harassing her. She's going to think you're a complete jerk."

Florian observed her across the room. "We're perfect for each other on paper. Two powerful families. Both gorgeous."

"Except you don't live your life on paper. You live it in the real world." I offered a sympathetic smile. "I get it, Florian. Women fawn all over you and you expect the same from Honey, but you're going to have to let this one go if you have any hope of attracting her in the future. Show don't tell."

His brow creased. "What does that mean?"

"It means just *be* awesome instead of telling her how awesome you are. Let her decide for herself." An image of Sheriff Nash flashed in my mind. He'd demonstrated his own awesomeness more times than I could count. I wasn't worthy of him.

I spent the remainder of the party sidestepping Castor and dodging attempts to discuss my rift with my aunt. Not exactly a great time. I did have a nice chat with Honey and decided I liked her even more. I sympathized with Florian, of course, because I loved him, but I didn't blame her for not being easily seduced by my cousin.

The party finally started to thin out and I seized the opportunity to head home. I took a different route through the woods, not wanting to get caught in a horde of witches eager to carry on with an afterparty. I needed a clear head tomorrow when I put my plan into action. Hopefully my newspaper trick worked or I'd have to start over with the list of suspects.

"Well done, my dear." My aunt emerged from the shadows of the tall live oak trees.

My stomach tightened. And here I thought I'd made it through the party unscathed. "Well done what?"

"I see you managed to catch the eye of an acceptable suitor. About time."

"Oh, Castor is deemed acceptable, is he?"

"Indeed. The Avens-Beech family is above reproach. I would've suggested him as a match ages ago if he hadn't been busy globe-trotting for his family's company."

Interesting that Florian hadn't mentioned our double date to her and that she hadn't ferreted out the information some other way.

"I'm surprised you're still interested in my romantic life. After all, I've been excised from the family. Seems to me you no longer have a stake in the outcome."

"You're a Rose. I will always have a stake in any outcome that involves you and Marley."

I gathered my strength. "It must kill you that you can't control that outcome."

She clasped her hands in front of her. "Can you truly blame me for wanting control of Ivy's magic? You're hardly a bastion of wise decision-making."

I didn't shrink from conflict and confrontation. It had been part of my job as a repo agent, not to mention a basic aspect of my personality. Still, there was something about conflict and confrontation with Aunt Hyacinth that unsettled me. Even Jimmy the Lighter didn't instill the same kind of fear in me as my aunt. Yes, she was powerful and terrifying, but so was he. It was more than that.

"You disapproved of my father's choices too. You disliked his choice of brides. I'm sure there's a list of other grievances. Your need to control and approve every decision is what drove him away."

Her expression remained cool and impassive. She could give a mannequin lessons on how to remain emotionless.

"Why do you want all that power for yourself?" I demanded. "What good do you do with any of it?"

"Good?" she repeated, as though I'd raised a foreign concept. "You act like I'm some cartoon wicked witch. There are no winged monkeys at my disposal, Yarrow."

"Ember. And you'd totally have flying monkeys if you could. Have you even asked yourself why you deserve this magic or have you grown so accustomed to having it all that you've stopped asking why?"

"You think too hard."

"And you don't think hard enough," I snapped. "You aren't actually powerful, you know. You only wield power. That's different."

"That's absurd."

"You don't even act in the best interest of the coven. You only act in the best interest of Hyacinth Rose-Muldoon. All that magic and you're still a selfish little girl who won't share her plethora of toys."

"I won't apologize for my good fortune."

"I'm not asking you to." I shifted my stance. "Only a truly brave paranormal can let go of their power. I guess you're not as brave as you think."

"Perhaps you should take those words to heart as well. Remember—you have Ivy's power now. You're in danger of being corrupted far worse than I ever was."

"Not likely. Unlike you, I don't think I deserve it. There's no sense of entitlement."

She sniffed and straightened. "I see we are once again at an impasse. I'll take my leave now. Good night."

I watched the darkness swallow her. Only when she was out of sight did I allow myself to feel. I collapsed against the nearest tree and choked back a sob. As much as I wanted to be tough and strong, it hurt to be rejected by her. My whole life had revolved around my dad until Karl entered the picture—and then Marley. Then my dad and Karl died and I figured it would be just the two of us for the rest of my life. Never did I imagine a secret family fervently searching for me.

When I was younger, I'd dreamed of a big family like the Waltons or the Bradys. Starry Hollow had been like the answer to a prayer I didn't realize I'd made. There were cousins and an aunt—an entire ready-made family had welcomed us to the fold. The money and prestige were perks, of course, but it had been the family that mattered the most. That connection to the father—and even the mother I'd lost. But Aunt Hyacinth's strings were attached to everything. She wasn't interested in Ember. She wanted Yarrow—the witch who'd been born into the family. She wanted the witch who would've been raised in Starry Hollow and learned to follow the rules set by her. But I wasn't that witch.

I'd never be that witch. She realized that now and decided I wasn't enough. Ivy's magic was worth more to her than our unconditional love. My tough exterior demanded that I deny the full extent of my heartbreak, but my interior finally betrayed me, pushing its way to the surface with the force of a tidal wave. I wrapped my arms around the tree and let myself cry. I ruined my makeup and probably managed to get a fresh set of twigs in my hair.

The wolf's steps were so silent that I didn't hear him approach until he was next to me. He nuzzled my hip and I tore my tear-stained face away from the bark to look at him.

"Well, this is embarrassing." Even in wolf form I recognized the sheriff. Despite the fur and sharp teeth, I recognized him the way a skilled musician recognized the notes to a song they'd never studied.

He nudged my hand and I crouched beside him so his head could nestle under my arm. "I'm okay. You don't have to shift back on my account. I was having a moment, but this too shall pass."

I'd likely interrupted his scheduled romp in the woods. Werewolves needed to run free in their animal shape every so often or the desire nagged at them until they exploded. For some wolves, it resembled pent-up aggression. For other wolves, it kept them in a constant state of discomfort until they were able to scratch the itch.

I leaned my back against the base of the tree and slid to a seated position. He settled his head in my lap. "You're like my emotional support animal." I stroked his neck, letting my fingers sink into the soft fur. I wasn't kidding. There was something incredibly soothing about petting an animal. My tears dissolved and the ache in my chest evaporated.

He gazed up at me and his bright eyes shone in the moonlight.

"You're too kind to me, Granger," I said. "I don't deserve it, not after how I treated you."

He licked my forearm as if to reassure me that wasn't true.

"I'm not crying over Alec." I dug my fingers deeper into his thick fur. "Thought you should know that. It's this fight with Aunt Hyacinth." I heaved a sigh. "I know you dislike her and probably think I'm better off without her, but she's family." Truth be told, I wanted a relationship with her. Yes, she was vindictive, arrogant, and ridiculously spoiled—but I believed she was also capable of genuine feelings. She could've cut Linnea and her werewolf children out of the family. Someone else in Hyacinth's position no doubt would've done so. But Linnea was still welcome. And Aunt Hyacinth adored Bryn and Hudson in her own way.

The wolf raised his head to check on me and I managed a smile. "I didn't expect to have such a strong reaction to seeing her, but I'm good now. Thanks."

He rose to all fours and trotted alongside me as I left the woods. I knew he was making sure I got back to my car safely. I should've arrived on my broomstick like everyone else.

"I have a wand and I'm not afraid to use it," I said. "Go ahead and finish your run. I'll be fine."

He gazed at me for a beat longer before turning back to the woods. I forced myself to continue to the car without looking over my shoulder. I knew he would come straight back if he thought I still needed him. Granger Nash was more than a wolf. More than a sheriff.

And I was finally beginning to accept he was more than a friend too.

# CHAPTER NINETEEN

TONIGHT WAS THE NIGHT. I'd driven around town and made sure there were newspapers in as many locations as I could think of. Fingers crossed the thief would see the article and fall for the ruse.

Today I spent in preparation. If my plan succeeded, I needed to contain the ring's power to stop it from spreading misfortune and that meant performing magic of my own.

I set a velvet pouch on my altar. One of the perks of Ivy's influx of power was that spells like this one seemed easier than before. I had to carefully follow the instructions, of course, but the magic itself was less draining and much more effective.

Florian peered over my shoulder. He'd come by to complain about Honey not returning his text and ended up as my assistant. I told him to let her go, but he wasn't a very good listener.

"Are you sure this is the right spell for what you want to achieve?" he asked.

"What's wrong with it?"

"It's a protective spell."

"It's sort of a reverse protective spell. I'm trying to protect the outside world from what's inside the pouch."

"But the pouch is empty."

"For now." If I played my cards right, there'd be a ring in it soon enough. "I need to neutralize the power of the object inside."

He smirked. "I don't think Mother will fit in there."

"This is the runway size," I teased. "I'm planning a larger version for her."

"She misses you, you know."

"She misses what I had to offer. She doesn't miss *me*."

"Believe me. I get why it seems that way. Sometimes she seems more like my boss than my mother."

"What did she say about Honey? She must've noticed you trailing after her at the party."

Florian squared his shoulders. "I was not trailing after her."

"It was like there was an invisible rope between you."

"You make me sound pathetic."

I shrugged. "If the rope fits."

I held the pouch in my bare hands and let the magic flow through my fingertips, caressing the soft fabric. I was acutely aware of each magical thread as it weaved its way through the velvet. The magic widened and wrapped around the fabric like a thick ribbon.

Conjuring the spell on the pouch was a step in the right direction, but it was only a step. Obtaining the ring in order to secure it in the pouch was quite another. I needed my plan to work before the town endured far worse than food poisoning, thunderstorms, and a power outage at the hospital. If the myth surrounding the ring was accurate, the stone had barely scratched the surface of the damage it could do.

"Whatever your client's paying you for all this time and effort, it isn't enough."

"He's my first client. I can't expect too much."

"That's part of your problem, don't you think? You don't expect much."

I eyed him. "What's that supposed to mean?"

He hugged me. "You deserve good things, Ember. You should expect more out of life."

I shook him off. "Now you're making me nervous." Florian wasn't a big hugger. Neither was I for that matter.

"What do you think I should do about Honey?"

"Exactly what I told you the last fifty times you asked. Stop texting and calling her. Let her decide without badgering her."

"Fine." He pulled out his phone and deleted her as a contact. "Consider it done."

"You have her in there twice, don't you?"

His expression answered my question. "What's she listed as Future Wife?"

"Smart and sexy," he murmured. He deleted the second contact. "What about Castor?"

"What about him?"

"Are you going out with him again?"

"I don't think so."

"What's stopping you? It's not like you're dating anyone else."

"Doesn't matter. I don't want to waste his time. He wants a wife and that wife won't be me. Now stop talking and let me finish. The fate of the world kind of depends on it."

I hefted the pouch from one hand to the other, mentally assessing the strength of the magic. If only there was a way I could test it beforehand. Unfortunately there wasn't anything powerful enough. I considered putting Ivy's wand in the pouch as an experiment. Aside from the fact it was too long to fit, I wasn't sure whether it would be a true test given that I was using Ivy's magic to complete the spell. A true experiment would involve a magical object unrelated to me. Oh, well. All that was left to do now was hope for the best.

As soon as the sun made its descent, I took off on my broomstick toward the cove. As prepared as I was for this confrontation, I still felt butterflies circling the pit of my stomach.

Careful to avoid hitting any branches on the way down, I landed in a clearing. I surveyed the area and decided on the best place to hide. I made sure to keep my broom within arm's length in case I needed to make a quick getaway. There was no telling how this might play out, not to mention the Council of Elders would be meeting later not far from here. I wanted to wrap this up before they interfered.

Crouching behind a bush, I awaited my prey. Was this what it felt like to be a lion stalking a gazelle at the watering hole? If so, it wasn't surprising that lions slept so much. Stalking was pretty dull work. I picked up a stick and wrote in the dirt—all work and no play makes Ember a dull girl.

After half an hour of shifting positions and repeatedly checking my text messages out of sheer boredom, an unfamiliar man wandered into view. Finally. I peered into the darkness to get a better look at him. Nope. Didn't recognize him. He seemed to be waiting for someone.

I emerged from my hiding spot. If he was an innocent bystander, I wanted to shoo him away for his own safety.

He blinked in surprise when he spotted me approaching. "Hey. Are you the one who left me the note?"

"Note?"

He produced a crumpled slip of paper from the pocket of his jeans. "You asked me to meet you here."

Before I could review the anonymous note, someone else joined our small party.

"What are you doing here?" a female voice asked, her tone laced with annoyance.

The man spun toward the voice. "Wanda?"

Sure enough, I turned to see the waitress from the restaurant.

"I told you I didn't want to see you anymore," he said gruffly.

Wanda flinched. "You don't mean that, Frank. We have a son."

"And I have a relationship with him, but that doesn't mean I need to have one with you. We're over. We've been over for ages. You have to accept it."

As much as I wanted to put the pieces together, I needed to get the ring, which wouldn't be easy with Frank here. The paranormal was a liability.

"Wanda, I need you to hand over the ring," I said.

Her eyes widened; she resembled a child with her hand caught in the cookie jar. "What ring?"

I opened my palm. "I know you stole Lindsey's engagement ring from the restroom and I know why. Please. You have no idea what you've done. I need that ring."

Wanda edged closer to the water. "I don't know what you're talking about."

She was still trying to complete the fake ritual. She must've lured her ex here in the hope of getting the ring to work right away.

"Wanda, what's this about? Did you write that note?" He pivoted to me. "And if she wrote the note, then who are you?"

"My name is Ember." I kept my focus on Wanda. "I hate to be the bearer of bad news, but the story about the ritual isn't real. I know because I planted it."

Wanda stopped inching. "It isn't real?"

I shook my head. "The ring isn't what you think. It won't do what you want."

Frank glanced between us. "Does anyone want to explain what's going on?"

Her eyes glimmered with hatred and anger. "You're lying! You're only saying that so you can steal the ring from me and use it for yourself."

Slowly I moved closer to her. "I recently ended a serious relationship with a vampire, Wanda. Trust me, even if the ring had that kind of power, I have no desire to claim eternal love. Change is part of life and the sooner we accept it, the happier we'll be."

Frank frowned. "Eternal love?"

"That's why she stole the ring," I explained. "She thought she could use it on you, so that you'd love her forever." I shifted back to Wanda. "But I swear to you, the ring has nothing to do with love. It's a story the family made up because they didn't know the real reason why their grandmother locked the ring away." But Nanny Berta knew the ring's origin, I was certain of it. She'd even tried to tell them at the hospital right before she died.

"Wanda, this is crazy," Frank said.

The fairy's enraged face was fixed on me. "You had no right!" She pushed out a wave of magic and it washed over me.

The force was so strong and unexpected that I lost my balance and stumbled to the side. I managed to catch myself before I toppled to the ground.

"Wanda, listen," I said.

But Wanda refused. Not satisfied with her first magical punch, she tried again. This time, the fairy used some kind of emotional magic. Intense sadness flooded my system. Tears swelled in my eyes and streamed down my cheeks.

"Wanda, stop," Frank pleaded.

I fought against the overwhelming emotions. She was using my own buried feelings against me. Apparently I suppressed a lot more sadness than I realized. If I weren't in mortal danger, I'd thank her for the release.

"Would you really have wanted to live an inauthentic life with me? Knowing that you used some stupid ring to make it happen?" Frank demanded.

"What's the difference between a magic ring luring you in versus fake boobs and a dye job?" she spat. "I'm sure you wouldn't object to those."

"Come on, Wanda. I know you. You're better than this."

I threw out my arms and expelled the fairy's magic.

Wanda reacted on instinct, using her magic to pick up a stone and hurl it at me. Unfortunately her aim was off and the stone whacked Frank in the side of the head. Moaning, he slumped to the ground.

"Frank!" She turned her full fury on me. "That was *your* fault!"

At this point I wasn't sure whether it was the ring's influence or plain bad luck. Either way, I had to subdue Wanda before she did any more damage.

"Listen to me," I said, trying to keep my voice calm. "The ring has nothing to do with eternal love. That was a myth. A story that got repeated so often, it became fact."

"You're telling me it's just a ring? I don't believe it. I can feel its magic."

"Yes, and that magic is destructive. It's called the Ring of Despair and it has a terrible history."

Her eyes flickered with uncertainty. "Despair?"

"It spreads misfortune. That's why Ben's grandmother kept it locked in a vault for decades. She knew of the ring's legacy but ignored it to her detriment. She lost both her husbands, including her first husband who was the love of her life."

That seemed to get her attention. "They died?"

"Yes, and ever since that ring has been back in circulation, bad things have been happening all over town. The food poisoning. The hospital."

She gasped and I saw the moment she realized the horrible truth.

"Yes, your son's illness too. The timing fits and you said the healers can't pinpoint a cause." I stretched out my hand. "Give me the ring, Wanda, and maybe we can heal him."

Her gaze flicked to Frank, still unconscious on the ground. "But a child needs both parents."

"And your son has them, just not in the same house." I sighed. "I get it, Wanda. I really do. I grew up without a mom. My daughter has grown up without a dad. I know you want to fight to keep your family intact, but it sounds like you were never a family to begin with."

Her eyes brimmed with unshed tears. "I got pregnant six months after we started dating. He broke up with me the night I was planning to tell him I was pregnant." She sucked in an emotional breath. "I've tried everything. I saw a therapist. She recommended no-contact, but you can't do that when you share custody of a child."

"There are potions…"

"I tried love potions, but nothing worked." She broke into a sob. "I can't seem to let him go no matter how hard I try."

"I wasn't going to suggest a love potion," I said calmly. "Another kind, one that breaks the connection and allows you to focus on your own healing."

She wiped away tears with the back of her sleeve. "There are potions that can do that?"

"Yes. You've been trying to use magic to control Frank's feelings instead of getting a handle on your own. I would suggest you recalibrate your mindset, if that makes sense."

Observing Wanda's conflicted emotions reminded me of my own. I had to trust myself to make decisions. This was my life now and it was time to fully embrace it.

"Yes," she said in a quiet voice. "That makes total sense."

"Giving up the ring is the best chance you have of healing your son," I said.

Physically and emotionally exhausted, she sank to her knees. "Ollie's my world. I'll do whatever you want if it means saving him." She tugged the ring from her pocket and tossed it on the ground at my feet. "Take it."

Like Dorothy's companions in *The Wizard of Oz*, it seemed that Wanda already had the one thing she'd desperately sought—eternal love.

I dug the velvet pouch from my purse and scooped up the ring. "Thank you, Wanda."

Frank stirred and she crawled over to him. Traces of smudged mascara underscored her eyes. "I'm sorry, Frank. No more of this, I promise."

He pulled himself to a seated position and touched the mark on the side of his head. "That's going to be quite an egg. Luckily we both know I have a thick skull."

She flashed a relieved smile. "You love our son and that's enough. I don't need more. Please forgive me."

He patted her hand. "You know I do. You're an amazing mother to Ollie. You'll always have a place in my life, it just can't be the one you want."

Wanda sniffled. "I didn't mean to hurt you."

"I know that." Frank looked at me. "What will you do with the ring?"

"That's up to the rightful owner. My only job was to find it."

And now my only hope was that they'd do the right thing.

## CHAPTER TWENTY

I PACED in front of the window, peering outside periodically.

"I thought you weren't supposed to conduct business out of the house anymore," Marley said.

"It's not business. Ben and Lindsey are friends coming over for tea." And if I happened to pass along a recovered family heirloom in between spooning lumps of sugar, so be it.

Marley threw herself on the sofa beside PP3, her fall cushioned by two plump pillows. "I wish Aunt Hyacinth would calm down. She's being ridiculous."

"She's angry because she's accustomed to getting her way and we've told her no." And a bully never liked being told no.

"Maybe we should move."

I stopped in my tracks. "Marley Rose, are you seriously suggesting we uproot ourselves from our familial home because some old witch is throwing a hissy fit?"

Marley fixed her blue eyes on me. "It's more than a hissy fit. She's doing real damage."

I moved to sit beside her and scooped the dog onto my

lap. "We're not going to react to her behavior by changing what makes us happy."

Moisture gathered in the corners of her eyes. "But you've already lost things that made you happy. Your job—and Alec."

I clasped her hand in mine. "I enjoyed working as a reporter, but it was only a job. There are always other jobs."

"What about Alec?"

"Love isn't always enough. And it isn't finite either. There's always more out there if you're open to the possibility." I squeezed her hand. "*You* are my priority."

"So that means you've decided to become a spinster hermit?"

"No, that means I do everything in my power to protect you and to lead by example, no matter the consequences."

PP3 lifted his head and prepared to scramble to the floor.

"I guess your clients are here," Marley said.

"My *friends*, you mean." Tucking the dog under my arm, I pulled myself to a standing position and ventured to the door.

Ben and Lindsey exited the car. The tension in their shoulders told me how anxious they were.

"Thanks for coming," I said, injecting a note of cheer into my voice to put them at ease.

Lindsey stroked PP3's head. "Hey, buddy. Aren't you sweet?"

The dog licked her hand. See, Aunt Hyacinth? Friends.

I ushered them inside the cottage and closed the door. Marley had already made herself scarce.

"Can I offer you anything to eat or drink?" I had the pot of tea ready just in case.

Ben slapped his thighs as he sat. "I'm too nervous to eat. I assume we're here because you found the ring."

I nodded toward the velvet pouch on the coffee table. "It was the waitress from the engagement party—Wanda." I told them the whole story.

"How is her son now? Is he better?" Lindsey asked. It spoke volumes that her first question was about the health of an innocent child. Ben had chosen wisely.

"He is," I said. "Once the ring was contained, the healers were able to make progress. He was discharged from the hospital last night."

Ben's face went slack. "This is horrible."

Lindsey shot him a quizzical look. "Honey?"

He buried his face in his hands. "If I hadn't taken the ring out of the vault, do you think Nanny would still be alive?"

Part of me wanted to lie to placate him, but I couldn't do it, not when there was still a decision to be made about the ring. "There's no way to know for sure."

"It seems like Nanny knew the risks," Lindsey said.

"Which is why she locked it away," Ben countered.

"The point is that she kept it," Lindsey pointed out gently. "She was a resourceful woman. If she'd wanted to dispose of it safely, she could've found a way. She didn't even mention it in her will or bother to safeguard it. What did she think would happen when she died?"

"And that brings us to next steps." I held up the velvet pouch. "You have three choices. I can give the ring back to you as requested."

Ben eyed the pouch warily. "What's the second choice?"

"I can try to cleanse the magic from the ring."

"And if it doesn't work?" Lindsey asked.

"I'll destroy it."

Ben frowned. "You can do that?"

"I don't know, but it's worth a try. There's enough misfortune in the world without a piece of jewelry adding to it."

Ben glanced at Lindsey. "It's your ring now. What do you think?"

"I vote for option two. If that fails, then destroy it. We can always find another ring for me, one that doesn't have negative associations."

"How will you know if it works?" Ben asked.

Even during the brief moment when the ring was on the ground at my feet, I'd felt the strength of its magic. "I'll know."

"What about the time it takes you to experiment?" Ben asked. "Won't the ring pose a danger?"

I jingled the pouch. "This is magically sealed. The ring holds no power while it's in here. I won't take it out when I use the spell."

Ben slid an arm along Lindsey's shoulders and squeezed. "Good luck. Let us know what happens."

"Ahem." Lindsey nudged him with her elbow.

"Right. I almost forgot." Ben removed his arm from her shoulders and dug into his pocket, retrieving a folded check. "Your payment."

"And we'll pay you again for your handling of the ring, whether you destroy it or cleanse it," Lindsey added.

Ben stood first and helped Lindsey to her feet. It was a sweet gesture and I wished them the best of luck with their marriage.

"Can I make a small suggestion?" I asked.

"Of course," Ben said.

I shifted my attention to Lindsey. "Your cousin, Kayla. Throw Bridezilla a bone and choose a different song for your wedding. She may be a narcissistic pain, but she's family."

Ben cut a glance at Lindsey. "What would you think of the theme song to that cat movie? The one that made us both cry?"

She kissed his cheek. "I don't care which song we dance to, as long as I'm in your arms."

I set PP3 on the floor and walked them to the door. "I'll be in touch." When I turned back toward the living room, Marley stood at the bottom of the stairs.

"She may be a narcissistic pain but she's family? For a second, I thought you were talking to them about Aunt Hyacinth."

"I guess every family has one."

"What time will Aster be here?" Marley asked.

I checked the clock on my phone. "Any minute."

*Oh, good. Then I'm right on time.* Raoul emerged from the kitchen with a drumstick clutched in his paws.

"You weren't invited. Where did you get that?" I demanded.

He tore off a piece of meat and chewed. *In the woods. Can you believe somebody left a whole bucket of these on a blanket?*

I smacked my forehead. "Raoul, they were having a picnic. They probably went for a hike and planned to come back to eat afterward."

He stared at the bone in his hand. *Oops.*

"Well, at least you only took one piece. They still have a whole bucket left."

He looked at me with an apologetic expression. *Oops.*

The honk of a horn alerted me to my cousin's arrival.

"Is that any way to summon me?" I asked, sliding into the passenger seat.

Marley and Raoul jumped into the backseat. "We're coming too," my daughter announced.

*I should be consulted on all decisions related to the business,* Raoul complained.

*Yes, you've made your position quite clear. Need I remind you the new office is closer to all fast food and pizza places?*

*And that's the only reason I haven't lodged a formal complaint with HR.*

I twisted to look between the seats at the raccoon. "We don't have a human resources department."

*Which explains my follow-up complaint about the absence of HR.*

"I can't wait for you to see this," Aster said. "You're going to love it."

My cousin didn't express strong emotions very often, but she was radiating with excitement right now and it was a joy to behold. Business ownership suited her. Maybe it would suit me too.

Aster parked in the nearby lot and we exited the car. The moment I laid eyes on the small building, I was transfixed. With its flower boxes and charming wooden exterior, it was so much more than a shed.

"Mom, this is great!" Marley raced ahead to open the door.

"I haven't even looked inside and I already know I'm going to be blown away," I said.

The interior was even more impressive. It was like Doctor Who's TARDIS, appearing to expand in size the moment we crossed the threshold.

"This is your work area." Aster tapped the top of a chair. "And that's Raoul's dedicated space."

The raccoon climbed onto a stool and rested his paws on the table. *It's perfect. I can fit a whole pizza box on here.*

I whirled around to face her. "Aster, this is incredible. I knew you'd create an amazing space, but this is next level."

My cousin beamed. "Thanks. It helps that I know you so well. I was able to tap into your needs and provide a space that suited your business as well as your personality."

"You're going to make a fortune with these," Marley said.

Aster perched on the arm of a chair. "I don't know about that, but I'm enjoying myself. The twins have shown an interest too, which is nice. They usually ignore whatever I'm working on."

"A future family business," Marley said.

"Speaking of family," I began. I hated to broach the subject, but it seemed necessary. "What kind of security measures can I put in place?"

"You can't ward the property because it doesn't belong to you," Aster said. "You can, however, ward the shed itself."

I couldn't imagine Aunt Hyacinth would stoop so low as to tamper with the shed, but at this point I couldn't rule anything out. She'd both surprised and disappointed me multiple times in recent months. At a certain point, I hoped she'd grow weary and move on to other grievances, but I knew it would take time. I'd recognized Ivy's magic was a big deal even before I acquired it. Now that it resided within me, I understood my aunt's desire to control it.

"I think I'll stay and conjure a temporary ward, just to have something in place." I'd come back another time and craft a stronger one. "I can walk home if you want to head out now."

"Who's in the mood for a treat?" Aster asked.

Raoul bounced off the stool like someone had offered him a lifetime supply of pizza. After they filed out of the shed, I took a moment to admire the various compartments for all my magical storage needs. Aster had clearly put a lot of thought into this.

The door clicked and I turned, expecting to see Aster again.

"Hey," I said.

Sheriff Nash stood outside the door holding a potted plant. "Hey, yourself. Thought I'd stop by with an...office-warming gift?"

I accepted the plant and moved it to the windowsill. "Thank you. This is so sweet."

He poked his head inside and examined the interior. "Nice setup you've got here. Aster did a great job."

"Thanks. Want to come in and see the rest?"

"Sure." He ducked inside and made himself comfortable on a stool. "Everything work out with your client?"

"For the most part."

He nodded. "Figured you'd manage. You've always been able to handle yourself."

"I'm officially open for business, so if you want to send any clients my way…" I motioned to the desk area.

"You'll be my first suggestion. I'll tell anybody willing to listen that even the most delicate matters are safe in your hands."

We stared at each other for a prolonged moment. If it had been anyone else, it would've been awkward, but Granger wasn't anyone else. Far from it.

"I feel like you're always going out of your way to be kind to me and you get nothing in return," I blurted.

He blinked rapidly. "Come again?"

"You brought a plant to my new office. I don't think I've even brought you a donut."

He pressed his lips together, as though deciding how to respond. "First, any acts of kindness I show you are not 'going out of my way.'"

"Sure they are. You have to go to the garden store, choose a plant, spend your money…"

He gave me a wry smile. "You found my father's killer, Rose. That trumps anything I've ever done for you. And you've done a million little things for me that could also be construed as 'going out of your way.'"

Lynda's remark echoed in my mind once again. *If you love*

*someone, let them go. If they return, they were always yours. If they don't, they were never yours to begin with.*

Although he didn't want to, he let me go when I made it clear it was what I needed. That was how much he loved me.

Gazing at him now, I felt a shift deep in my psyche. It was as though I was seeing him with a fresh pair of eyes. A shiver ran through me as I allowed a question to form in my mind —one I hadn't been brave enough to ask myself until now.

Had I finally returned?

\* \* \*

Read on for information about the next book in the series!

## ALSO BY ANNABEL CHASE

When a Bachelor-style reality show invades Starry Hollow and a contestant ends up dead, Ember is on the case—and the show. Be sure to preorder *Magic & Marriage*, the next book in the series, now. Also, if you haven't already, be sure to sign up for my VIP List at www.annabelchase.com and receive FREE bonus content, as well as information on sales and new releases.

### **Other series by Annabel Chase**

The Bloomin' Psychic

Spellbound/Spellbound Ever After

Federal Bureau of Magic

Crossroads Queen

Pandora's Pride

Midlife Magic Cocktail Club

Spellslingers Academy of Magic

Wings and Blades Academy

Divine Place

Magic Bullet

Printed in Great Britain
by Amazon